SECOND CHANCE WITH THE HERO

HEROES OF FREEDOM RIDGE

LIWEN Y. HO

Second Chance with the Hero

Scriptures taken from the Holy Bible, New International Version®, NIV®. Copyright © 1973, 1978, 1984, 2011 by Biblica, Inc.™ Used by permission of Zondervan. All rights reserved worldwide. www.zondervan.com The "NIV" and "New International Version" are trademarks registered in the United States Patent and Trademark Office by Biblica, Inc.®

Cover Design: Amanda Walker

ISBN: 9798357073396
First Edition

❀ Created with Vellum

My fellow Heroes of Freedom Ridge authors.
It's such a blessing to "work" with you! ;)

1

*J*osephine Gilbert hoped this would be the best Christmas of her life... just not her last one.

As soon as she pushed open the door to Stories and Scones, a strong sugary scent enveloped her, easing her worries. She loved the idea of this shop, combining two of her favorite things in the world—books and sweets. Josephine immediately felt at home. Seeing the woman waving to her from behind the buy counter quickly brought a smile to her face.

"Jan!" Josephine ran past several bookcases until she reached her dear high school friend. The two women embraced, then pulled apart to have a good look at each other. A couple of years had passed since she last saw Jan in person. Aside from her children and grandchildren, Jan was the one person she'd missed the most from her hometown of Freedom, Colorado. Having her within arm's reach now brought tears to her eyes. "I've missed you so much! You haven't changed at all!"

"You should talk!" Jan exclaimed as she shook her head of short hair. "You look like you stepped out of the pages of our

1

old yearbook. How do you not have any wrinkles? And your hair—there's not a single strand of gray. Whatever you were eating or drinking in California, I need a case of it—make that three!"

"Don't be ridiculous! I have plenty of wrinkles; I just like to call them laugh lines. And this color is all thanks to Clairol number nine." She laughed and tucked a lock of her shoulder-length blonde hair behind her ear. "*You're* the one who's glowing. Married life must be treating you well. How are you and Pete doing?"

"We're doing well, thank the Lord. We'll have to have you over for dinner soon so we can catch up. It's been too long, friend." Jan took her hand and patted it. She'd always been the nurturing type even when they were young. "It's so good to have you back. This is an answer to years of prayers —*years*, I tell you. I never gave up hope though that you'd come home."

Josephine nodded. "I know. Thank you for praying for me and the kids all these years."

"Don't even mention it. What are friends for?" Jan gave her fingers another squeeze as a young mom and her kids approached the counter. "Let me help these customers. Feel free to browse around. We have plenty of romance books that you'll love. I highly recommend the ones by Brandon Spark. You're guaranteed a happily ever after each time!"

Pasting on a smile, Josephine stepped aside. She stuck her hands into the pockets of her winter coat as she wandered the aisles. Her chest tightened when she passed the genre that Jan had mentioned. In the past, she would have grabbed a couple of them to take home to read by the fire. There'd been a time when she was a young stay-at-home mom with twins to take care of. During those long, exhausting days, she'd found refuge in fictional stories when romance in real life had been in short supply.

Oh, she'd been in love once upon a time. So in love that she'd gone against her parents' wishes and eloped with her high school sweetheart. That was nearly four decades ago. Now, at age fifty-nine, she'd been divorced for as long as she'd been married. A broken marriage had never been in her game plan, but it was what it was. She and Jack had married at twenty-one and become parents the year after that. Eventually, the burden and stress of raising a family had taken their toll on their relationship. They'd managed to last until the kids were almost out of high school.

Thinking back now, she couldn't pinpoint the exact moment when they'd grown apart. It was more a series of falling-outs. Little by little, she'd let disappointment and resentment burrow inside her heart until there was no space left for forgiveness. Not that she had ever stopped caring for Jack. Josephine would always have a place in her heart for the man who had shown her love in tangible ways that her parents hadn't. But even Jack's love had its limits.

Still, she was thankful that he had given her the two greatest gifts possible—their son and daughter. Jeremiah and Jess, as well as their growing families, were the reason she'd decided to sell her midwifery practice in California and move back to Freedom.

Now if only God would allow her to enjoy her retirement years with her loved ones by her side. This was her one and only prayer.

Ouch!

Josephine sucked in a sharp breath as pain overtook her right temple. The throbbing sensation immediately spread from her head to behind her eye. Everything around her blurred, making the covers on the picture books in her line of sight blend into a soup of colors and shapes. She grabbed onto the bookshelf, trying to stay upright through the dizzy spell that followed. Forcing herself to breathe, she prayed the same prayer she'd been praying for the past month since these headaches started.

Lord, I need more time. Please give me more time.

She'd already missed out on so many years of her grandchildren's lives. Video calls and brief visits weren't the same as spending consistent time with them in person. Now that they were all living in the same town, there was so much she hoped to do to make up for lost time. She'd been teaching ten-year-old Miah how to crochet her first hat, a blue one she wanted to give her dad for Christmas. Miah's five-year-old twin brothers, Adam and Asher, were expecting to bake cookies with her next week. She was supposed to be an extra pair of hands for Jess who was due with her second child at the end of this month. She'd already promised to take Jess's son Titus to the annual Christmas parade in two weeks. She couldn't fall ill now. Her throat tightened as tears threatened to fall. Shutting her eyes, she prayed and waited for the headache to pass... if it passed.

"Josephine! Are you all right?" Jan's usually upbeat voice was laced with worry. "Let's get you seated. Here we go. Easy now."

Josephine felt Jan's arm around her shoulder as she guided her to a nearby armchair. The moment she settled into the soft velvety fabric, a small weight lifted from her shoulders. At least this time she hadn't fallen. It had only taken one such incident at work to convince her it was time to retire.

"Are you okay?" Jan asked again. "You're as white as a sheet."

"I-I'm fine. A lot better now that I'm sitting. Thank you." She opened her eyes and tried to focus on Jan's face. "It's just a headache. I'll be okay in a little while."

"Let me get you some water. I'll call Jess, too, and let her know to pick you up."

"No, Jan—!" Josephine didn't get a chance to finish her sentence before Jan rushed off. The last thing she wanted was to worry her daughter, especially when she was pregnant. She had come to ease Jess's burdens, not become a burden herself. She'd do what she'd always done these past twenty years—take care of herself. That's how she'd lived her life since Jack left. With as much conviction as she could muster under the circumstances, she called out, "Jan, I'm fine, really! Please don't call Jess."

"Here, take this." Jan reappeared and carefully handed her a large mug. "It's your favorite."

Josephine guessed there was a tea bag in it based on the minty aroma wafting in the air. She couldn't believe that after all these years Jan still remembered how much she loved peppermint tea. Her friend's thoughtfulness warmed her as much as the heat from the mug did. It'd been a long time since anyone had taken care of her. "Thank you, Jan. I'm feeling better already. Please don't bother Jess with this. She has enough on her hands already."

"Too late. I already dialed her number—hi, Jess! It's Jan. No, I'm not calling about the scones you wanted. This is about your mother. Do you mind coming to the shop? She has a doozy of a headache, and I'd feel better if you could take her home." She paused for a moment. "No worries, we'll see you soon."

As soon as Jan hung up, she informed Josephine of the situation. "Jess is out buying diapers, but she'll come over as soon as she's done. In the meantime, you are to stay put."

"Fine." Josephine sighed. Jan's call had pretty much sealed her fate. She had no choice now but to wait. It was probably safer this way. Her headache wasn't getting any better and neither was her vision. She had a fairly high pain tolerance, but this ache was testing her limits. There was nothing she wanted more than to crawl into bed, something she planned on doing as soon as she got back to her apartment.

"How bad is it on a scale of one to ten," Jan asked, "ten being the worst?"

"Depends on your definition of worst."

"Childbirth's a ten in my book. Is it as bad as that?"

"It depends on who you're asking." Josephine winced and closed her eyes. In her former line of work, she'd seen it all. From quick deliveries with minimal pushing to long, drawn-out labors that bordered on intolerable. Regardless of the intensity or length of childbirth, its pain bore fruit. This headache had no purpose but to render her defenseless.

"You're looking worse and worse by the minute, Josephine. I think we should get you to the ER."

"No! I'll be fine after a nap, really."

"How often have you been having these headaches?"

"That depends on your definition—"

"Josephine Gilbert," Jan cut her off with a frustrated tone, "talk to me. I'm trying to help you, but how can I help if you keep dodging my questions?"

Josephine didn't need to see her friend's face to know she wasn't having any more of her games. To be honest, she didn't have the strength for them, either. She could barely hold her mug. "Can you take this?"

Once her hands were free, she turned onto her side and curled up into a ball on the armchair. She dug the toes of her boots into the carpet as she forced herself to take slow, deep breaths. Her headaches had never been this bad before. Maybe it was time to admit she needed medical attention.

"Nine and a half," she eked out through gritted teeth. "I've been having them for a few weeks."

Jan gasped. "Josephine! You should've seen a doctor already! What if it's what your mom had?" Her tone softened as she insisted, "I'm calling Pete and we're taking you to the ER."

Josephine didn't argue this time. If she could, she'd drive herself to the hospital. Hearing Jan speak her fear out loud only added to her anxiety. Her mother had nearly passed from a ruptured brain aneurysm around this same age. She'd had all the telltale symptoms—headaches, blurry vision, dizziness—for months. After seeing what her mother had been through, she should have known better. But between retiring and the move, she hadn't had time to see a doctor. She'd meant to make an appointment once she'd settled in here, but she'd been too caught up this past week spending time with her grandkids. No more excuses. She just hoped it wasn't too late.

Please, Lord, give me more time. She offered this prayer as if her life depended on it because it did. Surely the One who knew the number of hairs on her head could protect what was inside her thick skull a little longer. Just long enough so she could tell her family how much she loved them. Maybe even long enough so she could make amends with the one person she had wronged in her life.

It was likely out of desperation, but for the first time since her divorce, she made this request of God: *Please give me a chance to talk to Jack.*

2

*J*ack Gilbert knew a dire situation when he saw one.

As a medic on an oil rig off the coast of Angola for nearly two decades, he thought he'd seen it all. Various kinds of fractures, contusions, dislocations, and burns. And more cases of tooth decay than he cared to remember. But the symptoms that today's patient presented with had him breaking out into a sweat.

"How long did you say you've been feeling ill, Wendy?"

The woman in her early forties opened her mouth to answer, then immediately clamped a hand over her lips. She lurched off the exam table, grabbed the nearest trash can, and buried her face in it. The retching sounds that followed resonated off the white sterile walls of the sickbay.

Jack knelt beside her and held her long brown hair back. He said a prayer for Wendy, asking God to bring relief to her queasy stomach. His heart went out to her, partly because she reminded him of his daughter Jess who was just a few years younger. He also felt an extra burden when caring for the women who worked on this rig. There were only a handful who had ventured into this world that had previously been reserved for men. They were equally as brave and smart as their male counterparts, but they had to work extra hard to prove themselves.

He offered Wendy a handful of tissues when she finally let go of the trash can.

She accepted them with a weary smile and wiped her mouth. "Thank you. I'm sorry about this mess."

"Don't worry about it. Let's get you off the floor." He helped her onto the exam table before taking a seat on the stool beside it. "Now, tell me again how long you've been sick, and have you had any other symptoms?"

"It's been two days. I thought it was the lasagna from the other night—I don't do well with too much cheese—but it's only been getting worse. I can't keep any food down, sometimes not even water."

"Any fever or chills?"

"No. It's not like a regular flu or cold. I don't know what's wrong. I've never felt this bad before."

He'd only met Wendy ten minutes ago, but he took her word for it. Her complexion had grown paler since she'd stepped inside the room. "Let me take your vitals and we can go from there."

After taking her blood pressure and temperature and doing a quick exam, Jack was only more puzzled. Nothing looked out of the ordinary. He almost wished Wendy had a fever; at least that would confirm the presence of a virus. The other condition he suspected was food poisoning, but with no one else on board experiencing the same symptoms, he ruled that out as well. What could this be?

He prayed for wisdom from above. Having worked in medicine all these years only confirmed how finite his knowledge was. The human body was complex, intricate, and amazing. He only understood a small fraction of what its Creator knew. He racked his brain, considering what other possibilities could be at play.

"Where were you before this hitch started?" he asked. They'd only started their current offshore period of service five days ago. If this bug had an incubation period similar to that of the stomach flu, Wendy would have caught the virus on land. Which meant this could be one of any number of contagious illnesses. "Can you tell me all the places you visited last week and who you were with?"

"I was home in California. It was just me, my husband, and our dog. We mostly stayed home except for our daily walks."

Jack's ears perked up at the mention of the Golden State. There'd been a time when he'd contemplated moving there in hopes of saving his marriage. He still regretted not following through on that impulse. Knowing what he knew now, he'd have done everything possible to repair his relationship with Josephine—

He sucked in a sharp breath. That was it! He had a hunch what Wendy might be suffering from.

"Is there any possibility that you're pregnant?"

Wendy's mouth fell open. "P-pregnant?"

"Yes. When my wife—ex-wife—was pregnant with our twins, she had the same kind of nausea. It was like what you described—she couldn't keep anything down, not even water."

Her hands flew to her stomach as she stared down at her navy sweatshirt. "Did you say twins?"

"I'm not saying *you're* pregnant with twins, Wendy, but if you are pregnant, you could be experiencing morning sickness. The name's obviously a misnomer since some women can have it all day." He walked over to one of the overhead cabinets and pulled out a small rectangular box. Handing it to Wendy, he instructed her, "Why don't we see what this pregnancy test says?"

Eyes still wide, she took the test and entered the bathroom adjacent to the office.

While Jack waited, his gaze fell upon a framed photo on his desk. The image frozen in time was from a Christmas long ago back in his hometown. In those days, he'd worked long hours as a paramedic to make ends meet for his young family. He remembered getting off early that particular year so he could attend the tree lighting ceremony with Josephine and their son and daughter. Jeremiah's and Jess's blue eyes had lit up at the sight of the gigantic tree that had towered over their small five-year-old frames. The mayor of Freedom had taken their picture while they stood under the light snowfall, huddled together for warmth. The four of them then snacked on hot chocolate and peppermint bark, a decision they later regretted when the twins had the hardest time falling asleep due to the sugar high.

He smiled at the fond memory. Those were some of the best days of his life. When he and Josephine had no one else to rely on but each other. When the kids were still young and innocent. Before his hours on the job were cut due to union rules and their finances got tight. And before Josephine decided to ask her wealthy parents for money. That had been a sore point in their marriage. It wasn't that he'd been too proud to ask others for help, but to ask the very people who had looked down on him for his poor background was too much. But maybe if he hadn't let his pride get in the way, he wouldn't have lost his family.

If only he'd realized this twenty years ago.

The bathroom door opened, drawing Jack's attention back to the present. He looked up to see Wendy holding the pregnancy test with a small smile on her face.

"You were right. It's positive."

Jack noted the two lines on the test, one a little lighter than the other but still evident. What a relief. It was as he'd suspected. "Congratulations, Wendy! We found the cause of your illness. You're going to have a baby!"

"I'm going to have a baby," she repeated with wonder. She placed a hand on her midsection and shook her head. "I can't believe it. The doctors always told me I couldn't get pregnant. I stopped praying for a miracle a long time ago."

"That doesn't mean God stopped working," Jack reassured her. "Come on and have a seat. Let me get you some ginger ale and crackers to help with the nausea. Then we'll arrange to have you medevacked to the nearest hospital to meet with an OB. You'll want to talk to your supervisor about the rest of this hitch as well as the upcoming ones."

"I will. Thank you so much."

An hour later, Jack watched as Wendy boarded the helicopter to fly to shore. He returned to his office, praising God for blessing his patient as well as keeping everyone else on the rig healthy and safe. This was his prayer often, especially during the holiday season when these workers were away from their families. The kitchen served special meals for them, but good food could only do so much. Turkey and apple pie were a poor substitute for the company of loved ones. The one thing you could count on when you worked away from home was growth—children growing up and couples growing apart. He understood the sacrifice all too well.

At a quarter after five, he finished typing up his patient notes. He took off his bifocals and rubbed his eyes, ready to call it a day. As the only medic on the rig, he was still on call after hours, but he could go about his own business. He planned to work out in the gym, eat dinner, and make some video calls to his kids. Thankfully, he had repaired his relationships with Jeremiah and Jess because there was nothing he enjoyed more than being their father and now a grandfather to their children.

Ring!

His cell phone rang with an incoming call. The area code on the screen read 303; he recognized the Colorado number as Jess's. It was too early for her to be calling though. "Hello, Jess? Is everything okay?"

"Daddy?" His daughter's voice came over the line, breathy and quavering. She sounded like she was on the verge of tears. "Daddy, I'm so scared."

"What is it, sweetheart? Are you hurt? Where are you?"

"At the ER. It's Mom. She's—" A sob choked off the rest of her words.

Jack shot up from his chair. "What about Mom? What happened to her?"

Jess stopped crying long enough to utter a couple of sentences. "She's in so much pain. I don't know what to do."

His heart about stopped. "Was she in an accident? How serious is it? I need more details, Jess."

"I was out shopping when Jan called. She asked me to pick Mom up because she had a headache. By the time I got to Stories and Scones, they'd called an ambulance. I followed them here as fast as I could. I only saw Mom for a second, but she didn't look good at all. I don't know what's wrong. How could a headache be this bad?"

Jack's head spun with all the information. As far as he knew, Josephine didn't get migraines. Unless her health had changed in the twenty years since he'd last seen her, which it very well could have. He wasn't privy to her personal details anymore, but he desperately wanted to know more.

"Can you find out who's treating her? I want to talk to the doctor." Silence followed, tightening his chest. "Jess?"

She suddenly cried out in pain. "Oh no. Not now."

"Sweetheart, are you okay?"

"I'm fine. Just having some contractions. Hopefully they're Braxton Hicks. But I guess if they're real, this is the best place to have them."

He jumped to his feet. This situation was getting more desperate by the minute. *Lord, what can I do?*

Go home.

Jack blinked. He didn't hear an audible voice, but the message was the same one he'd been sensing in his heart for the past few months. For far too long, he'd been wanting to return to Freedom. There had always been an excuse—legitimate or not—to keep him from going. But no more. He needed to be there for his family. He would need to pull some strings to get an early leave, but he'd do whatever it took. His kids and grandkids needed him. Josephine needed him, too.

At least he prayed she would accept his help.

3

---

*J*osephine breathed freely for the first time since she'd entered the hospital. For some unknown reason, the pain in her head had subsided, leaving a more manageable ache in its wake. She thanked the Lord for this much-needed reprieve. At the moment, she could see and think clearly again, but the nonchalant look on the ER doctor's face had her feeling confused. He didn't seem concerned at all about her symptoms.

"Mrs., uh, Gilbert, is it?" The dark-haired man who looked nearly young enough to be her grandchild stared at his clipboard and jotted down some notes. His white coat matched the color of the walls in the small exam room.

"It's *Ms.* Gilbert," she replied, more annoyed at herself than at the doctor. She should have changed back to her maiden name of Walton years ago, but she'd never found a good opportunity to do so. All the bills and accounts were under her married name, so she reasoned it was easier this way. But every time someone addressed her, she was reminded of the fact that she was no longer a Gilbert. Not since the heartbreaking day those divorce papers showed up in her mailbox.

A much smaller pile of paperwork appeared before her eyes as the doctor waved them in front of her face. "Here are your discharge papers. If you have no other complaints, Ms. Gilbert, you're free to go."

"That's it? Are you sure I don't need any tests done?"

"I don't see the need now that you're feeling better. You said yourself that you've been under a lot of stress moving back to Freedom. Tension headaches are very common. There could also be hormonal changes at play considering your advanced age."

Her jaw dropped. Perhaps tact wasn't part of the curriculum for Bedside Manner 101. "I already went through menopause four years ago, thank you very much. I hope when you said advanced, you meant mature."

He laughed nervously. "I see your humor is returning; that's always a good sign. You take care of yourself, Ms. Gilbert. If you have any other concerns today, feel free to come back. I likely won't be here if you do, but you can ask for my supervisor, Dr. Palmer." Without a further word, he scurried out of the exam room like a rabbit on the run.

Josephine frowned. So much for wanting help. Here she had let herself be dragged to the hospital and she was no better off than when she'd arrived an hour ago. The situation had seemed so dire during the ambulance ride, she'd imagined the worst-case scenario. While she was thankful for this other outcome, she didn't want to go through anything like that ever again. What she needed were answers, and she was determined to get them.

But first, to find Jess.

She'd only heard her daughter's voice call out to her as she boarded the ambulance, reassuring her that she'd meet her here. Josephine had wanted to let her know it wasn't necessary, but she hadn't had the strength to reply. She only hoped Jess wasn't too worried about her; she certainly didn't need the extra stress. She already had her hands full with little Titus. He was at that age where he loved to run and explore and test limits, which often resulted in Jess chasing after him. Josephine could only imagine how adventurous he could become in this new environment.

She gingerly stepped down from the exam table and gathered her purse and coat. After heading down a hallway to her right, she stepped out into the waiting room. For a small town like Freedom, the ER was unusually busy on this Thursday afternoon. She spotted several mothers with their young ones in tow, likely here with flu symptoms from the looks of their flushed, feverish faces. The sight made Josephine even more anxious to urge Jess and Titus to go home.

She recognized her daughter from the red winter coat she wore. With one hand on her lower back, Jess used the other to hold onto Titus as they stood at the receptionist's desk.

Josephine quickly made her way over. "Jess! I'm done. Let's get you and Titus home."

As soon as Jess turned around, her expression softened with relief. "Mom! I was so worried about you! Are you okay?"

The two of them embraced with Titus sandwiched in between their legs. When Josephine pulled back, she saw Jess's eyes well up. She wiped away the tears that spilled down her daughter's pale cheeks. "I'm fine, sweetie, just fine. I'm sorry for worrying you. Let's hurry up and get out of here. There are too many germs here for my liking."

"What did the doctor say? Did they find out why your headache was so bad?"

"He said it was likely stress. I'm sure a good night's sleep will do the trick."

"But Mom, did they do any tests? What if you have what Grandmother had? Aren't brain aneurysms hereditary?"

"Not always," she answered, even though the statistics stated otherwise. She'd done plenty of research after her mother's incident to know that one was four times more likely to have an aneurysm if a first-degree relative did. But she didn't want to worry Jess over probabilities. It was hard living with a constant rain cloud over your head, wondering if and when you would be affected. She'd had firsthand experience with that. All she was sure of was that their futures were in God's hands, and He had a reason for everything that happened.

That was enough certainty for her.

"The doctor said I can always come back if I need to. But now what I want is to get you and Titus home. Where's Titus?" Josephine's heart sank when she didn't see his head of curls. When had he run off and where did he go? "Titus?"

Jess spun around, her hands on her head. "Titus, baby, where are you? Has anyone seen a little boy? He's two and about this tall—" she gestured to the height just below her growing belly "—with blond hair and blue eyes."

The dozen and a half people occupying the waiting room chairs shook their heads. Josephine was about to ask the woman at the front desk to block off the exits when she heard a man calling out.

"Anyone looking for a little boy?" The man wearing glasses and a white doctor's coat gave them a friendly smile as he walked over. He held a squirming Titus who was busy pulling on the stethoscope hanging around his neck. "I found him by the fish tank."

"Mommy!" Titus cried out as he reached for Jess. "I saw fishies! Lots of fishies!"

"Oh, sweet boy, you need to stay close to Mommy. Please don't run off again." Jess sighed. "Thank you, doctor, for finding him. He has the hardest time being still. He's just so curious about everything."

"No worries. Curiosity's not a bad thing. It'll take him places, you'll see."

"Hopefully not too far away from me, at least before he knows his way home," Jess joked. She raised her brows, then glanced at Josephine. "Doctor, do you mind checking my mom out? She had a horrible headache and my dad said she should get an MRI to rule out a brain aneurysm. We have a family history of it."

Josephine's throat constricted, making it hard to swallow. "Jess! You talked to your father? You shouldn't have called him. Look at me, I'm fine. I don't understand why you had to call him."

"I was scared, Mom! I didn't know what else to do. I wanted to talk to someone with a medical background, and he was the first person I thought of. Daddy still cares about you, even though you guys aren't together anymore."

Mortified, Josephine clamped her lips together. She noticed a few patients craning their heads as inconspicuously as possible to hear more of their conversation. Thankfully, she didn't recognize any of their faces. This wasn't the time nor the place to be broadcasting the demise of her marriage. She'd faced enough shame twenty years ago when she became a single mom.

"Excuse me for interrupting," the doctor spoke up, "but you mentioned a family history of brain aneurysms?"

"Yes," Jess continued, "my grandmother—my mom's mom—had one that ruptured."

"We should definitely do an MRI then. Let me pull up your chart, Mrs., uh…"

"Gilbert," Jess supplied. "It's Josephine Gilbert. Age 59, blood type O, shoe size seven and a half."

"Good to know." He chuckled. "I'm Dr. Palmer. Age 32, blood type B positive, shoe size nine. Why don't you ladies take a seat? I'll give the Radiology department a ring and find out when they can fit you in."

They walked to the nearest chairs and sat down. An activity cube on the table in front of them caught Titus's attention and he climbed down Jess's lap to examine it. Josephine made sure to keep her eyes trained on him at all times. They'd already had enough excitement for one day.

Jess placed a hand on her arm. "I hope you're not too mad, Mom. I didn't think you minded me talking to Daddy about you."

Shaking her head, Josephine answered, "I'm not mad, sweetie, just a little caught off guard. I..." Her voice trailed off as she contemplated how to verbalize her concerns. "Your father has his own life now. He really doesn't need to be bothered with something like this."

"But I'm sure he wants to know what's going on with you. You guys were married for almost twenty years! That's a long time."

"And we've been apart for just as long, even longer if you count all the time he was away for work before the divorce. We haven't seen each other or even talked in I don't know how many years."

She and Jack had been forced to interact in the years following the divorce, but it had always been to discuss matters related to the kids. After Jeremiah and Jess were on their own, the glue that had kept them in each other's spheres dissolved. Josephine didn't know anything current about Jack, except for what Jess told her. The last photo she'd seen of him was years ago. She often wondered if she'd recognize him if he showed up on her doorstep.

"Just consider it a blessing to have another person praying for you, Mom."

"Y-your father's praying for me?" Her throat was so dry, the words almost got stuck. The idea that her ex-husband would do such a thing floored her. They hadn't parted on the best of terms, and the last time they'd talked, she'd been less than gracious. How could he have forgiven her so easily?

"Of course. He said he'd pray all the way over here. I don't think he was exaggerating either."

Josephine's gaze darted to Jess's face for the briefest of seconds. The mischievous smile she saw worried her as much as the time she'd found the twins playing with a jar of peanut butter. She had a sinking feeling she didn't want to know the answer to her next question, but she had to find out. "What do you mean by 'all the way over here'?"

"Daddy said he'll pray for you during his flight from Angola to Denver. That's close to seventeen hours!"

"Jessica Davina Gilbert Franklin!" She quickly got down on the ground beside Titus so she could keep him in sight while she faced her daughter. "What did you say to your father to make him want to hop on a plane?"

"I didn't say anything, Mom. He was the one who offered to come home."

Home. Did Jack consider Freedom his home anymore? He hadn't been back in decades. And now he was coming back for her? Preposterous didn't even begin to describe this situation!

Josephine took a deep breath to calm herself. "Jess, I need you to call your father back and tell him not to come—"

Ring!

The familiar tune of a Christmas carol filled the air.

"That's mine!" Jess rummaged around in her coat pockets until she pulled out a cell phone. One glance at the screen made her brows shoot up. She held the phone out to

Josephine with a glint in her bright blue eyes. "Here, Mom, you can tell Dad yourself."

Josephine's stomach dropped. She only had one thought —God sure had answered her prayer quickly. Here was her chance to talk to Jack.

4

ack was in such a rush to pack up his things, he hadn't had a moment to sit down in the past hour. After meeting with his supervisor and negotiating an early leave from this hitch, he placed a call to Jess to let her know his plans. He'd only heard her say "hello" when he started talking.

"Hi, sweetheart, it's Dad. I just booked a red-eye from Luanda that leaves at ten tonight. There weren't any direct flights, but I managed to find one with a five-hour layover in Frankfurt. I should be arriving in Denver around four in the afternoon tomorrow, your time. I'll get a rental car so don't worry about picking me up. Are there any updates on Mom? Where should I meet you guys?"

The silence that followed made him freeze. His whole body tensed as a wave of fear washed over him. Why wasn't Jess answering? Had something happened to Josephine? Jack slumped onto the twin-sized bed in his small living quarters. He forced himself to take a deep breath and mentally prepare himself for the answer to his next question. "Am I too late, Jess?"

"Jack."

His throat grew raw. The female voice was more mature than Jess's and oddly familiar, but he couldn't believe his ears. He hadn't heard Josephine's voice since the last time he saw her in person at Jess's wedding; that was close to a dozen years ago. To be able to hear her now, especially to hear her say his name, felt like a gift from God. "Joey, is that you?"

A pause followed before she answered, "It's Josephine."

"Yes, Josephine." He'd forgotten that he no longer had a right to call her by the pet name he'd starting using when they were teens. "How are you feeling? Did the doctors say what's wrong?"

"I'm better. The doctor wants to do an MRI, but it's just a routine procedure. I appreciate your concern, Jack, but you really don't need to come."

"But Jess said you were in a lot of pain and then she started having contractions. I want to come back to help in any way I can."

"Jess! You're having contractions?" Josephine's voice grew emotional as she addressed their daughter. "Why didn't you tell me? How far apart are they? We should get you upstairs to Labor and Delivery to get checked out."

"It was a false alarm, Mom," Jess spoke up in the background. "They stopped as quickly as they came. What about Daddy? When is he coming home?"

"He's not." Josephine repeated her request to Jack. "Please cancel your flight. Jess and I are both doing fine now. There's no point in you making a trip halfway around the world for nothing."

"It wouldn't be for nothing. I want to see Jess and Jeremiah and our grandkids. I'd like to see you, too." Once Jack spoke that last sentence out loud, he realized how much he meant it. He missed his family, especially Josephine. Even if she was doing well now, he still wanted to see her. The possibility of a health scare made it clearer than ever that he couldn't let more time go by before making amends. If God had given him this opportunity to go home, he would not let it go to waste. "I'm long overdue for a visit to Freedom. I already got the time off and I'm just about done packing. I'm good to go."

Silence fell over the line, followed by a soft sigh. "Well, if you really want to come back, I can't stop you. But don't do it on my account. I don't have much time to socialize these days. I just moved back to Freedom and there's still a lot of unpacking I need to do. And with Jess having her little one in a few weeks, I'll be busy helping her watch Titus."

"Ti-Ti!" a little boy's voice called out in the background. "That's me!"

"Yes, I'm talking about you, sweetheart." Josephine's tone brightened, holding a trace of a smile in her voice. "He is the cutest little boy, but a handful, let me tell you. I can't take my eyes off him for one second. Reminds me of someone—"

"Definitely not me!" Jess cut in, her voice loud and clear on the other end. "I'm sure you were going to say Jeremiah, right, Mom? *I* was a perfect angel!"

"Hm-hmm. You keep telling yourself that," Josephine joked. "My memory's not that bad yet, sweetie. I still remember the time you convinced your brother to dye the dog's hair blue."

Jack smirked as he recalled their family's first pet, a playful Maltese. "With a Sharpie, no less! Q-Tip looked like a Smurf for weeks."

"Yes, poor Q-Tip. After that, he always ran away at the first sight of a marker."

Shaking his head, he remarked wryly, "Those were some fun days, weren't they?"

"Fun and exhausting."

"Exactly. What was that phrase you used to say? Something about the days being long…"

"The days are long, but the years are short."

"Yes, that's it. It's crazy how fast time has flown by." He ran a hand across his jawline, feeling the stubble there. The small mirror on the wall across from him reflected the gray in his facial hair and sideburns. "How is it that we're old enough to be grandparents? Sometimes I don't even recognize my own reflection."

"You know what that means, don't you?"

"What?"

"It's time you got new glasses," she quipped, not missing a beat.

"Ha!" The laughter that emerged from his lips came from his gut, loud and free. Jack couldn't remember the last time he'd let go like this. "That's a good one. You always did have the best sense of humor."

"That's only because you were always so easily amused."

Jack grinned. It felt like old times between the two of them. Why had he waited so long to reach out to Josephine? Suddenly feeling bold, he decided to take a chance. "Here's an idea. I'd be happy to help watch Titus with you. I'm sure with two pairs of hands and eyes between us, we'll have no problem keeping him out of trouble. We were always good at tag-teaming. What do you say, Joey?"

Her end grew quiet, making Jack's gut twist. Had he said too much, too soon? Perhaps he'd gotten too comfortable, especially with using her nickname again. He was about to apologize when Jess's voice came over the line.

"Hey, Daddy, can we call you back? The doctor's taking Mom to get the MRI now."

"Sure, of course. Please call me as soon as you get the results."

"Will do."

He paused, wishing he could talk to Josephine more about his offer, but that would have to wait. "Please tell your mom I'll keep praying for her."

"I will, Daddy."

Jack started praying as soon as the call ended. He continued throughout the next hour during his helicopter ride to the mainland, then the taxi ride to the airport in Angola's capital city. Each passing minute felt like an hour of waiting. He lost track of how many times he checked his phone to see if Jess had called back. It wasn't until he was sitting outside the boarding gate did his phone ring. It wasn't his daughter's but his son's somber voice that greeted him.

"Hey, Dad. Jess needed to take Titus home and get him to bed, so I told her I'd call you back."

"Jeremiah, thanks for calling. How's your mother doing?"

"As usual, there's good news and not so good news."

Jack's mouth grew dry. "What's the bad news?"

"Mom has a fairly large aneurysm about the size of a grape. They're recommending surgery, either tomorrow or the day after, depending on when they can fit her in."

"Surgery? As in brain surgery?"

"Yes. The procedure will essentially cut off the blood flow to the aneurysm and keep it from rupturing. She's checking into the hospital tonight so they can prep her as soon as there's an opening. I'm filling out the paperwork right now."

He ran a hand down his face, suddenly feeling weary. On one hand, he was thankful the doctors had caught the aneurysm when they did. On the other, he couldn't bear the thought of Josephine being operated on. He'd had a hard enough time watching her recover from her C-section with the twins. It'd taken a toll on not only her body but her mind. He imagined the process of healing from brain surgery would be even more taxing. "You said there was good news. Now would be the time to hear it."

"Well, the good news is that the aneurysm hasn't ruptured. The doctor said he's never seen one this big before. He called Mom a walking miracle."

Jack's lips parted in a small smile. Truer words had never been spoken. He'd always known Josephine was a miracle —*his* miracle. From the moment they met freshman year in math class, she had been a tangible proof of God's grace in his life. She had offered him love and acceptance when no other classmates would give him a second glance. He still recalled how she'd given him school supplies he hadn't been able to afford—a notebook and a mechanical pencil—and how she had also gifted him with the sweetest smile. He'd fallen fast and hard for that kind-hearted blonde-haired, blue-eyed girl. Even now, so many decades later, she still had a hold on his heart.

"She's a miracle indeed," he remarked as he swiped at his eyes. Sadness weighed heavily on his shoulders. *Is it too late, Lord, to let her know how much she means to me?* He hoped and prayed it wasn't. "What did the doctor say about the recovery period? How long will she need to stay in the hospital?"

"She'll be in the ICU for a week. A full recovery will take anywhere from four to eight weeks. We'll know more after the surgery is done."

"Okay. I'll come straight to the hospital after I land. Veteran's Memorial, I presume?"

"Yes, but about that, Dad." Jeremiah cleared his throat. "I don't know if it's a good idea for you to be coming to see Mom."

"Do you mean at the hospital or at all?"

"At all. Hear me out, Dad. I know you want to come and help, and we honestly could use the extra hand, but the doc says Mom needs to take it easy and be under as little stress as possible."

"Which is why I *should* come," Jack insisted without hesitation. "You and Jess have your own families to take care of, so my coming back is as much for you guys as it is for your mom. I can give her the time and attention that you guys can't."

"I appreciate that, Dad, but we have to think about what's best for Mom. The two of you haven't talked in ages. A hospital room isn't the ideal place to reconnect. She'll be in a lot of pain after the surgery, and you know how Mom gets when she has to rely on other people to do things for her."

"Stubborn and particular? Oh, I remember." He shook his head as old memories came flooding back. There was the time when Josephine had twisted her ankle and he'd offered to take care of the household chores. She'd reluctantly written out detailed instructions for him on how to do every single task, even the seemingly easy ones—or so he'd thought. He'd realized too late that he should have followed her instructions on how to sort the laundry. "Don't worry, I learned my lesson. The next time your mom gives me instructions on how to do something, I promise to follow them to a T. Especially if it has anything to do with separating the reds from the whites."

Jeremiah groaned. "I forgot about that. I had to wear pink socks to all my softball games. Haven teased me about them for weeks."

"And look at the two of you now, married with three kids."

A soft chuckle came over the line. "I'm pretty sure it wasn't because of the socks. I think God's grace had something more to do with it."

"I know." Jack couldn't be happier that his son had grown into a mature man of God, especially after the tumultuous period he'd gone through as a teenager. He certainly couldn't take any of the credit. Despite his shortcomings and failures as a parent, God had blessed both of his children so richly. It was all grace—unmerited and divine. He had experienced the same favor himself. That's why he longed to be the hands and feet of Jesus for others, especially his family. "I hear everything you're saying, son. I understand your concerns. But I want to do this for your mom. I wasn't there for her when she needed me before, but I can be there for her now."

"All right, Dad, but try to give her some space. Let her come to you for help. She needs to learn to trust you again."

Jack blinked in surprise. He never imagined getting relationship tips from his son, but it was spot-on advice. "How did you get so wise?"

"Unfortunately, from making mistakes," he replied wryly.

"That's what mistakes are for, to learn from. And trusting in God to redeem them."

"Sounds like my old man has gotten wiser, too."

He smiled. "I'm working on it. Better late than never, right?"

A female voice came over the loudspeaker, interrupting their conversation to announce, "Flight 1012, departing for Frankfurt, Germany, will begin boarding shortly at gate seven."

"Hey, Jeremiah, it's time for me to board. I'll see you soon. Tell your mom I'll be praying for her during my flight."

"I will. Safe travels, Dad. We're all praying—Haven and the kids, too—for you and for Mom. Who knows, this might be the most memorable Christmas in Freedom Ridge yet."

For better or worse, Jack was sure this holiday would be one for the books. But his sincere prayer was for a Christmas filled with good, positive memories. With the way he'd failed his marriage and his kids, he owed his family that much.

5

*J*osephine now understood the metaphor of feeling like you'd been hit by a truck. She thought she'd known exhaustion before as a mother of newborn twins, but the tiredness overtaking her body now was like nothing she'd ever experienced. Not only was she tired, but she also felt weak. With her limbs wobbly like Jell-O, her mouth as dry as cotton, and her head aching, she wondered if she did in fact get struck by a car. Her heavy eyelids refused to budge as she lay on her back. Where was she? What had happened?

She racked her brain to recall her last memories. Bits and pieces appeared like the parts of a puzzle, joining together to form a mental picture. Jess and Titus waving goodbye and blowing her kisses. Jeremiah handing her a backpack of clothes. Her friend Jan sitting by her bedside. Tossing and turning all night in an unfamiliar bed—the hospital! That's right. She'd checked in and they'd gotten her labs drawn to prepare her for surgery.

Had she had the surgery already? She dragged her right hand off the bed and lifted it ever so slowly to her head. Her fingers grazed some cotton bandages where her hair should have been. She sucked in a breath. Had they shaved her whole head?

"Good evening, ma'am," a cheerful female voice greeted her. "Careful now with your head. I'm Nancy, your post-op nurse. How are you feeling, Mrs. Gilbert?"

Josephine didn't bother correcting her. Any speaking that required more than one-word answers was out of the question. She channeled what little strength she had into opening her eyes. The first image that came into view was of Nancy's short black hair and her red and green—likely Christmas-themed—scrubs. Without her glasses, everything around her appeared like in a haze. It was rather appropriate given how fuzzy her brain felt, too. Having been an RN before she became a midwife, she had learned the aftereffects of general anesthesia. Experiencing it firsthand, however, was a whole different story.

Wetting her lips, Josephine attempted to form an answer. Half her face felt like it was still asleep. Only a whisper emerged, one that was barely audible over the beeping of the machines in the room. "Fine."

"The doctor said your surgery went as expected," Nancy remarked as she came closer. "I'll go ahead and check your vitals."

Josephine said a prayer of thanks that all had gone well. The hardest part was over. She closed her eyes to shut out the bright light in the recovery room. She disliked playing the role of patient, but she knew these measures were necessary. Her pulse, oxygen level, temperature and blood pressure all needed to be stable before she could be transferred to the ICU.

"All right, everything looks good," Nancy announced after a few minutes. Her voice mingled with the familiar scratchy sound of velcro coming apart. "Blood pressure is 132 over 80."

Josephine's chest tightened. Something wasn't right. Why hadn't she felt the blood pressure cuff wrapped around her arm nor its squeezing motion?

Her eyes flew open to find Nancy on her left side, placing her arm back down on top of the blanket. An arm she could no longer control. "My hand," she uttered, her words coming out slurred, "I can't move it!"

Nancy pulled back a large corner of Josephine's blanket to reveal the bottom half of her pale blue hospital gown. "What about your leg or foot? Can you try moving them?"

Using all her focus and might, Josephine urged her limb to cooperate. *Come on, you can do it!* Despite her best efforts and the internal pep talk, she couldn't even wiggle a toe. The gratitude she'd felt only minutes ago vanished while despair took its place. "What happened?"

"This sometimes occurs after brain surgery." Nancy pulled the blanket back over her legs. "I'll let the doctor know, but he'll likely say this is to be expected. The hospital will get you set up with occupational and physical therapy once you're discharged."

Josephine forced herself to breathe. There was no use in panicking, as much as she wanted to. But it was hard not to think of all the worst-case scenarios. Issues she hadn't considered before suddenly became insurmountable obstacles. For one thing, she lived on the second floor of a building that was only accessible by a staircase. If she couldn't walk, how would she be able to get to her apartment? What was worse, how would she be able to care for her grandchildren if she couldn't help herself? Her vision blurred even more as hot tears gathered in her eyes. The last thing she wanted was to be alone right now. "Is my family here?"

"Oh yes, there's a gentleman who's been waiting for you to wake up. He went to the cafeteria a little while ago to get coffee. I can check if he's back yet."

The weight on her shoulders lifted a little. Jeremiah had mentioned he'd return after the surgery to check on her. He had grown into a solid man of faith since his youth. She hoped he would provide some words of encouragement for her. "That's my son."

"Your son? You're nowhere near old enough to be that man's mother! I assumed he was your husband. Or boyfriend, perhaps? I see you're not wearing a ring."

Josephine stilled as a storm of emotions washed over her. "How old is he?"

"I'm so bad at guessing people's ages. Maybe in his mid to late fifties? I heard a couple of the nurses call him a silver fox."

Her stomach turned as she realized whom Nancy was referring to. "Not my son."

"Yeah, I didn't think so. Who is he if you don't mind me asking?"

"My ex."

"Oh!" Nancy harrumphed. "He's not here to cause trouble, is he? If so, I can get security to escort him out."

"No, don't." She knew Jack wouldn't hurt a fly, at least not physically. Emotions, however, were a different matter; she knew that firsthand. But time had closed up the wound in her heart. She still had a scar to show for it, but the pain had become a distant memory. Distant enough that she believed she'd be okay being in the same room with him again. But right at this moment? Her pride wasn't quite ready to take a beating.

"Do you want me to send him back here?" Nancy asked, her tone cautious. "If you're not ready to see him, I'll tell him you need your rest and to come back another day."

Josephine didn't mean to be vain, but she had to ask, "How bad do I look?"

"Not bad, but I know what will help." Nancy gave her hand a pat. "Did you bring any makeup with you?"

"In my backpack."

Nancy retrieved her small makeup bag and looked inside. "Let's see what we have here. Ah, yes, this will do."

After applying a coat of pink lipstick, Nancy gave her a good once-over and nodded her approval. "Some blush and eyeshadow would be nice, but since you have some bruising around your right eye, I'm not going to touch anything else on your face. This'll have to do. Unless you want to go heavy and dark. I was an expert at Goth makeup during my high school days. I'm sure I still have the skills to pull it off."

Josephine managed a small smile. "It's good. Thank you."

"Think nothing of it. Oh, I almost forgot. Be right back."

When her nurse slash fairy godmother returned, she brought with her a floral scarf. "The doctor didn't shave off too much of your hair, but if you prefer to cover up your head, you can use this."

"Sure."

Nancy loosely draped the scarf over Josephine's head and tied the ends together at the nape of her neck. She then held her cell phone up to allow Josephine to use the camera app as a mirror. "What do you think?"

The fuzzy reflection reminded her that she was legally blind without her bifocals. "My glasses."

"Where are they? In your bag?"

"Outside pocket."

"Got it."

A moment later, everything came into focus for Josephine. First, the room with its sterile white walls and the array of medical equipment by her bedside, then Nancy's youthful, smiling face. She took a deep breath, feeling more grounded now that she could see clearly again. But the instant she glimpsed her image on the screen, her chest tightened. The woman staring back at her looked more ready for Halloween than a reunion with her ex-husband. Her pale complexion accentuated the redness of the bruising along her hairline. And the deep weariness reflected in her eyes aged her a dozen years. There was no denying that she'd be making an impression on Jack—a very bad one! She couldn't let him see her like this.

"I can't."

"Not ready to see him? No problem. I'll tell him to come back—"

"Knock knock. Mind if I come in?"

Josephine froze as Jack's deep, velvety voice filled the room. The familiar sound sent a rush of heat through her body. The sensation dismayed her. How could she still have such a strong reaction to someone who was no longer part of her life? Maybe it was due to shock or embarrassment at her current state. Whatever the reason, she pushed aside the confusing feelings clouding her heart. Jack was here for their family, nothing more.

Except that he wasn't.

He'd come to the hospital to see *her*. Was it out of obligation or guilt, perhaps? Whatever the reason, she couldn't ignore the man, not when he was already here. With great reluctance, she lifted her gaze to where he stood in the doorway, filling it with his commanding presence.

She swallowed hard. Jack was even more handsome than the last time she saw him, which was saying a lot, considering he'd been dressed up in a tuxedo on the day of Jess's wedding. Silver fox, indeed. His wide shoulders filled out the black winter coat that he wore over a white button-down shirt. Strands of gray streaked the sideburns of his sandy brown hair and along his beard, giving him a dignified appearance. Lines appeared at the corners of his amber-colored eyes as he smiled. For someone who had just traveled around the world, Jack looked awfully put together. Too put together in her opinion. Why did he have to age so well?

Nancy glanced at Josephine with a questioning look. "Is it okay?"

Josephine nodded. Being alone with Jack was far from okay, but she couldn't avoid him anymore. She was a grown woman, for crying out loud. One who'd been ordering off the senior menu for several years now. She would face her ex-husband with grace and dignity—or go down trying.

6

*J*ack forced himself not to react to the sight of Josephine lying so helplessly in the hospital bed. Every cell in his body yearned to rush over and gather her up in his arms like he once had, but he remained calm. As calm as he'd learned how to be when he'd worked as a paramedic in Freedom. In those days, he'd show up at the scene of a crash and push aside his worries and fears. That was the only way he got his job done. But this was not an emergency call that needed to be answered nor was Josephine a patient who needed his attention. The woman before him was family. Perhaps not in a way that the law recognized, but she would forever be the mother of his children. For that reason, and many others, he would treat her with the respect and care she deserved.

The respect and care he should have given her long ago.

When Jack reached her bedside, he lost his train of thought for a moment. Even in her weakened state, she still possessed an air of grace and elegance. He was completely mesmerized by her high cheekbones and long lashes, along with those full pink lips. She was still as beautiful as the day he first laid eyes on her. He took a seat in the chair that the nurse had vacated and raised his gaze to meet hers. "Hey, aren't you a sight for sore eyes."

"You mean fright. I've had better days."

His chest tightened, hearing Josephine's slow and slurred speech. He schooled his expression so as not to worry her. Squeezing out a smile, he shook his head. "You're as radiant as ever, Joey—Josephine," he corrected himself. "I'm sure I wouldn't look half as good as you after having brain surgery."

"It's a good thing I'm the one who had surgery then."

He couldn't repress his laughter. Her dry wit always surprised him. "You haven't changed at all. You're still as funny as the day we met. Tough, too. How're you feeling?"

"Good."

"Yeah? They must have you on some strong meds for the pain."

She pursed her lips, likely too tired to reply. Her right hand grasped the edge of her blanket, bunching it between her fingers. She focused her attention on the movement as she murmured, "I thought I told you not to come."

Jack blew out a breath. It was more a statement than an accusation, which was an improvement from their past exchanges. Still, he sensed the mood in the room shift. "You did say that, but you know me, listening's not exactly my strong suit," he quipped, hoping to keep the conversation light.

"You haven't changed much either."

"Yes and no. I hope I'm wiser than the man I was twenty years ago. I'm definitely a lot grayer and more wrinkled if you haven't noticed."

"I noticed. Other people have, too."

"Other people? Who do you mean?"

She nodded toward the doorway where two middle-aged

women wearing scrubs stood whispering to each other. When the nurses realized they'd been spotted, the red-haired one stepped into the room.

"Sorry to bother you. I'm Angie and this is Charlotte," she introduced the two of them. "Could we get your autograph?"

Jack was so taken aback by their request, words failed him. "I-I'm sorry?"

"Your autograph," Angie repeated with enthusiasm. "You're the actor from that Hallmark movie, right? The one where the high-powered attorney goes back to her hometown for Christmas and bumps into her old flame. You played the old flame! I know it's you; I just watched it last week."

Jack held a hand up. "No, no, I'm afraid you're mistaken. I'm not an actor, just a medic visiting Freedom for Christmas."

"Are you sure?" Angie's shoulders drooped, reflecting her great disappointment. "How can it not be you? You're so handsome and charming! You should really think about going into show business. There aren't enough mature men in those movies. You'd make the perfect leading man. Wouldn't he, Char?"

Charlotte nodded eagerly, her brown eyes never leaving Jack's face. "So perfect."

"That's very kind of you to say," Jack replied, "but acting's not a skill the good Lord gifted me with."

"That's too bad." After a sigh, Angie's countenance suddenly brightened. "If I can't have your autograph, can I get your number instead? I don't see a ring on your finger, so I'm assuming you two aren't an item."

Jack wondered if he was so tired from traveling that he was dreaming. Were women usually this forward? Certainly not the ones he worked with on the rig. First, an autograph, and now his number? He needed to put an end to this nonsense.

Ahem!

Before he could speak, Josephine cleared her throat just loud enough to break whatever spell the two nurses were under. They fixed their attention on her at once, both offering their services.

"Is there something you need, ma'am?"

"What can we do for you?"

"A heat pad, please," Josephine murmured. "I have chills."

"Oh, you poor thing!" Angie exclaimed. "I'll go get one."

"I'll bring you a cup of hot water," Charlotte added. "That'll warm you up."

"Thank you, ladies," Jack called out to the women as they hurried out. He immediately turned to face Josephine as worry weighed on his chest. "Want me to get you another blanket?"

She smirked. "No, I'm fine. I only said that to help you out."

It took a second for her words to register. He ran a hand through his hair, thoroughly amused. "Did I look like I needed help?"

"Did you not?"

Jack saw a smile playing on her lips. "What are you smiling about?"

"You still don't get it, Jack."

"Get what?"

"The effect you have on women."

"What are you talking about? The nurses mistook me for someone else. Whoever that actor is—he's the one they wanted to ask out."

"If you say so."

Jack didn't know what to make of her vague response. This topic of conversation reminded him too much of their

44

last one at Jess's wedding. The one they'd had outside of the reception hall when they unexpectedly crossed paths after having avoided each other the entire day. He still recalled Josephine's fiery expression and the emotions brimming in her voice.

What are you doing with that girl, Jack? She's young enough to be your daughter!

She's just a friend. Jess had no problems with me bringing her today.

Just a friend? Really? Don't you care what other people think? All our relatives and friends are talking! They say you're going through some kind of midlife crisis, and I don't disagree. It's embarrassing, Jack.

I don't care what they say or think. I don't have to answer to them or to you anymore. Thanks for your concern, Josephine, but I know what I'm doing.

If you say so.

In hindsight, Jack had in fact known quite clearly what he was doing. He'd purposely brought a date to their daughter's wedding, knowing full well that Josephine would be there. It wasn't so much a midlife crisis as an ego crisis. He'd wanted to show everyone, especially his ex-wife, that he'd moved on and was doing well. In reality though, he'd been struggling with regret and doing everything he could to make himself feel better. Fancy clothes, an expensive watch, and a young, attractive woman—they were part of his new identity. The identity he had put on to help him forget his failures as a husband and a father.

It'd taken him a long time to forgive himself for the mistakes he'd made. He wondered how long it would take Josephine to forgive him, too—if she ever would.

"Jack?"

"Yeah?" He noticed Josephine looking at him expectantly. "Sorry, did you say something?"

"What time is it in Angola?"

"Right now?" He checked his watch which was still set to West Africa Standard Time. "Almost two in the morning."

"You should go get some rest."

"I'm fine. I rested my eyes on the plane."

"You don't look fine. I mean, you look better than fine—that's beside the point." She blew out a breath as her cheeks reddened.

Jack furrowed his brows, surprised to see her flustered. The Josephine he knew was as strong and unmoving as a lighthouse in a storm. Perhaps this was a side effect of the surgery?

"The point is," she continued, "I can tell you're tired. Your eyebrow twitches when you don't sleep enough."

As if on cue, Jack felt a spasm in his left brow. He reached up to massage his temple. "You're right. As always," he added with chagrin.

"Not always, just most of the time." She punctuated her statement with a small smile, adding a slight sparkle to her tired eyes. "Go on now. You need to rest."

"All right. I should let you get some rest, too." He glanced around the room and spotted Josephine's belongings. With just a small bag, she likely had brought only the essentials. Knowing how much she liked to stay active, he imagined she would need some entertainment. "Is there anything you want me to bring for you tomorrow? Some books or music? Maybe something to eat?"

"Thank you, but no. I appreciate you coming, Jack, but you don't need to come again."

"I don't mind at all coming back to keep you company. How else will you pass the time in here?"

"I have books on my phone. The kids will come by. I'll be sleeping, too. I'll be fine."

As frail as Josephine appeared, she was sure insistent.

Jack had to give her credit for that. Once she made up her mind, she stuck by her decision. She'd always been that way. He knew the more he tried to push, the more she'd stand her ground. That's why he'd finally conceded all those years ago when she'd given him an ultimatum—if he didn't quit his job, she would file for divorce. He'd gotten tired of all the fighting, so he'd gone ahead and done the deed for her. He never thought she'd actually sign the papers though.

He'd learned his lesson. If Josephine didn't want him to come back, he'd respect her wishes. As Jeremiah had said, he needed to give her time to trust him. Even though his mind knew this, his heart wished otherwise. It took everything in him to keep his emotions out of the situation.

Rising to his feet, he nodded. "I'll be staying at Freedom Ridge Lodge if you need to reach me. Take care of yourself, Josephine. It was good seeing you."

With one last smile, he left his ex-wife's side and prayed he'd have another chance to see her again.

7

*J*osephine couldn't help chiding herself for the slip of the tongue she'd made in Jack's presence. *You look better than fine.* What had she been thinking when she admitted how attractive she found her ex-husband?

She clearly hadn't been thinking.

She'd been exhausted and weak and obviously still affected by the anesthesia, not to mention the brain surgery itself. It must have been a combination of those factors that had made her recall everything she had once loved about Jack. How charming he was without any pretense. He had never let his popularity go to his head, not even when he eventually won over the hearts of their entire class and was voted Homecoming King. She appreciated how he treated everybody equally and never looked down on anyone. He was patient, gracious, and sacrificial. That was so refreshing to see, especially in comparison to the way her attorney parents had lived.

Her mom and dad had been all about laws and verdicts and winning every case, no matter how cutthroat they had to be in the courtroom. The very thing that had disqualified Jack in their eyes—his servant's heart—was what had driven her to elope with him. She remembered it all too well, the emotions of those early days when they were so deeply in love with each other. And the more she'd tried to tell her heart not to feel, the more it betrayed her.

But now that a week had passed since the night Jack had visited her in the hospital, she could think more clearly. Some people thought distance made the heart grow fonder, but in her case, Jack's absence made her heart tougher. Without his kind smile or soothing voice to distract her, Josephine could see the situation for what it was—a dream. It was the "what could have been" version of her and Jack's marriage.

The reality was that he had left her and the kids to chase a paycheck.

Footsteps sounded at the doorway as her daughter's voice filled the room. "Mom? I just filled out the discharge paperwork. Are you about ready to go?"

Josephine turned away from the window of her private hospital room and saw Jess leaning against the frame of the door. At three weeks shy of her due date, she looked about ready to pop. Her belly was much larger this time around than during her first pregnancy and her expression even more weary. "Just about. Come sit for a bit. Your brother said he's running late."

Jess made her way slowly over to the chair beside Josephine's bed and sat down. Only the top two buttons of her red coat were fastened, revealing the green Christmas sweater she wore beneath. "Did he say when he's coming? Duncan's working the night shift, so I need to be home by five. Or else he's going to have to bring Titus to the precinct."

"That's in half an hour," Josephine remarked as she

looked at the clock on the wall. "You should go on home. I know Ti-Ti wouldn't mind going to work with his daddy, but I'm not sure a car seat is meant to go in the back of a patrol car," she joked. "Jeremiah should be here soon. He said he had a surprise delivery planned for Haven and wanted to be there when she received it." She suddenly gasped. "Oh my goodness! I completely forgot!"

It was at this moment that Josephine realized what day it was—December twelfth—and its importance. Today was her children's birthday as well as Haven's. It was also her son and his wife's wedding anniversary. Her stomach dropped. What a terrible mother she was! How in the world had she forgotten these important occasions?

"It's okay, Mom!" Jess replied. "It's not a big deal. You've had so much on your plate this week. And anyhow, it's not like we're kids anymore. We don't expect anything for turning 37. Growing old is a gift in and of itself. We can always celebrate another day. Duncan says I can pretend it's my birthday again tomorrow since he can't be home tonight."

Josephine was touched by Jess's wisdom and graciousness, but she couldn't shake her guilt. "I know, sweetheart, but this wasn't how it was supposed to go. I had plans to make each of you your own cake. I already bought your gifts; I just need to wrap them." She sighed, looking down at her hands. While she had regained some feeling and movement on her left side, she didn't have full use of it yet. Overall, her recovery was moving along at a good pace, and for that she was thankful. But her condition had sure put a damper on this whole day. "I can't believe I ruined it for you all. I'm so sorry. I promise to make it up to you and Jeremiah and Haven, too—"

"Mom, relax!" Jess cut in with a laugh. "I know you're the queen of planning, but things happen. Please don't feel bad at all. We're just happy and relieved that you're okay. You getting well is the best gift we could ask for. And having Daddy back, too. As far as I'm concerned, this is one of the best birthdays I've had in a long time."

Josephine smiled. Her daughter might be a grown woman, but she could still hear traces of the little girl she once was. There'd been a time when all Jess had wanted was to have Jack home for Christmas. Work on the oil rig had kept him away for months at a time. They didn't always have the funds for him to fly back, especially with all the kids' sports equipment and music lessons they had to pay for. Not to mention their clothes and shoes, which they kept outgrowing. While Josephine understood that Jack had taken the job to support their family, his decision had turned their family life upside down. And the worst part was that he hadn't even talked to her about it.

There was no use dwelling on a past that she couldn't fix. But she could make up for her current mistake.

"Thank you for understanding, Jess. I'm going to do all I can to get myself back on my feet. There's so much I want to do with all the grandkids before Christmas. And I plan on keeping my promise to Titus to take him to the parade."

Jess wrinkled her brows. "Um, Mom, you do realize the parade's next Friday? I don't mean to be pessimistic, but one week of physical therapy's probably not going to cut it. Not to mention you'll be too worn out from the therapy to do anything at night. I'll ask Haven and Jere to take Titus. He'll enjoy spending time with his cousins."

"No, I can do it!" Josephine winced at the volume in her voice. Even she couldn't deny the desperation in her words. She wanted to believe she was being optimistic, but the one person she could never lie to was herself. Her stubbornness was her strength *and* her downfall. With a heavy heart, she stared down at her frail body and sighed. She might be dressed in comfortable sweats and sneakers, but there was nothing comforting about her current state. Lifting her gaze to meet Jess's, she admitted, "You're right. I don't think I can keep up with Titus at this point. I hope he won't be too disappointed."

"Don't worry, Mom, he'll understand. He'll be happy just sitting on your lap and having you read him a book. If you're up for it, I can bring him by this week some time to visit you."

"Of course I'll be up—" Josephine held her tongue when she saw Jess quirk a brow. "How about I see how I feel and let you know?"

"That sounds good."

The grin that Jess fought to hide made her eyes roll. "Why do I feel like our roles have reversed?"

"Never! You will always be older and wiser than me, Mom."

"Emphasis on older." Josephine smirked. "All right, go home to your boys. Give Ti-Ti a kiss from me."

"Will do!" Jess offered her a quick hug. When she pulled back, she released a deep sigh. "I wish you'd reconsider staying at our place. I'm worried about you, Mom. How are you going to manage on your own?"

"The same way I've managed all these years. I'll be fine, sweetheart. Jan stocked my fridge with enough food to feed a small army. And I have my new set of wheels"—she pointed to the gray folding walker by the bed—"to get me around. Your brother will be coming every other day to take me to therapy, so if there's anything I need done around the apartment, he can help me."

Buzz!

Josephine's cell phone vibrated with an incoming call. Jeremiah's name flashed across the screen. "Speaking of your brother…"

"I'll get going. Give me a call when you get home, Mom!" Jess added before she disappeared through the door.

Josephine answered the phone with her working hand, "Hi, son."

"Sorry for the delay, Mom. I'm on my way now. I should be at the hospital in ten minutes."

Hearing the tiredness in her son's voice made her heart ache. He had so much on his plate with his job at a security firm and also raising three young kids. Having to shuttle her around only added another layer to his responsibilities. "There's no need to apologize. If anyone should apologize, it's me. I completely forgot today was the twelfth. I'm so sorry, sweetheart. You should be at home celebrating with your family, not playing chauffeur for me."

"Think nothing of it, Mom. I'm happy to spend part of my birthday with you. Haven and I celebrated at lunch with the kids. Now I get to celebrate again with you at dinner. What could be better than that?"

Josephine had several answers for that question, all of which involved Jeremiah being at home with his family. In fact, the more she thought about the situation, the more frustrated she became. She never wanted to be a burden to anyone, least of all her children. They had already suffered enough when they were younger. Jeremiah, especially, had taken the news of her and Jack's divorce hard. She couldn't ask with a clear conscience for her son to sacrifice even more.

What other options do I have?

She considered asking Jan for help, but her dear friend had already taken time from her busy schedule to shop and cook for her. This was also one of the busiest times of the year for the bookstore.

What can I do, Lord?

As soon as she'd prayed, a name came to her.

Jack.

He'd come all the way from Angola to see her. Not only that, he was literally back in Freedom with no plans—assuming he hadn't gotten corralled into going on a date yet. She'd been secretly pleased he hadn't taken the bait the other night when the nurse had asked for his number. Not that she had any say in whom he dated, but it was a nice surprise to see that he hadn't been swayed by a pretty, younger woman.

But that wasn't important right now. She needed to address the situation at hand.

"Jeremiah, go back home, son. Haven and the kids need you. I'll find someone else to come get me."

"Mom, I'm already halfway to the hospital. It's not a problem at all. I'd rather be the one to take you home than have a stranger do it. Jess wouldn't want that either."

"It won't be a stranger." She released a shaky breath. "I'm going to call your father."

Once the words were out, there was no going back. Josephine said a quick prayer, asking God for courage. She could do this. For her kids' sake, she'd humble herself and ask Jack for help.

8

*J*ack glanced over at the passenger seat of his rental car, still not quite believing whom he had the pleasure of driving home tonight. Miracle of miracles—God had answered his prayers.

"I'll admit I was surprised to hear from you," he stated casually, trying to strike up a conversation. Josephine hadn't said a word other than *thank you* since she'd gotten into the car. Jack felt his chance to reconnect with her quickly slipping away. "Don't get me wrong, I was very happy you called. I just didn't expect it."

"It was a bit of a surprise for me, too, to be honest." She cleared her throat and shifted in her seat. "I actually lost track of the days while I was in the hospital, so I didn't realize it was the twelfth."

"You mean the kids' birthday?"

"Yes. I completely forgot their birthday. On top of that, it's also Jeremiah and Haven's anniversary. I couldn't take him away from his family today of all days. That's why I called you. I still can't believe I dropped the ball like that."

The dejected look on Josephine's face wasn't one he was

used to. She seemed like a shell of the woman he had seen a week ago. Even then, despite her being so frail after the surgery, she'd put on a strong face. Right now, everything from her slouched posture to her quiet voice made him realize how much she was beating herself up over this memory lapse. "You're being much too hard on yourself, Josephine. I'm sure the kids understand. They're more concerned with your recovery than anything else."

She sighed heavily. "I still feel bad."

Jack's fingers itched to reach over the center console and take Josephine's hand in his. There had been a time when he would have done so without a second thought. In fact, they used to hold hands so often in the car, he'd become an expert at driving with his left knee if he happened to be holding a drink at the same time. It wasn't a skill Josephine appreciated since she thought it set a bad example for the kids. Nevertheless, she didn't stop holding his hand...

...until one day she did.

Now that he thought about it, it was around the time he'd taken the oil rig job. The physical distance between him and Josephine eventually became an emotional distance they couldn't overcome.

Why didn't I realize what was happening, Lord? If I had, I could have done something to fix it.

It's not too late.

That same still, small voice seemed to whisper in his heart, giving him a boost of hope. He knew God's grace was so much bigger than any mistake he had ever made or could make. Jesus's death and resurrection had already paid for all his sins—past, present, and future. What he needed now was wisdom to know how to support Josephine through this difficult time. And to have patience—so much patience. He couldn't afford to mess up this time.

"You were there for every single one of their birthdays

when they were growing up. Not to mention all the holidays, too. That counts for something," he reassured her. "You definitely get the Best Parent of the Year Award in my eyes. It's no secret the kids liked you more than me."

"Not all the time."

"Come on. Most of the time then."

Josephine chuckled, her mood seeming to lighten. "Okay, I won't argue with that."

Jack stopped the car at an intersection, giving him a chance to meet Josephine's eyes. His throat tightened when their gazes locked. Her beauty mesmerized him. She was like a fine wine whose aroma and quality had improved with time. He felt like a tired, old man next to her, but one with a ticker that still beat strongly. Placing a hand on his chest, he was surprised to find his heart rate picking up speed. A flash of heat filled his body, warming him better than the hot air coming from the vents. Maybe he wasn't as old as he thought, not with his body behaving like a teenager's.

"What's wrong, Jack? Are you feeling okay?" Josephine asked, her voice laced with concern.

He stepped on the gas as the light turned green. "Nothing's wrong."

"Are you sure? You were holding your chest. Did you have an arrythmia? You used to get them all the time when you didn't sleep enough."

"I'm fine, really." As much as he enjoyed having Josephine care enough to fret over him, he didn't want to worry her. "It wasn't that. My heart rate was just a little fast, that's all."

"That's all?" she repeated, not sounding a bit convinced. "When was the last time you had a physical and bloodwork done? We're getting older, Jack. We have to be more mindful of our health. You can't put off taking tests like you used to do."

"I'm perfectly healthy, I promise." He couldn't reveal the

real reason behind his body's reaction, so he tried to change the topic. As they entered the downtown area, they came upon some of their old haunts on Main Street. He gestured to the storefronts that were decked out with holiday lights and decor. "It's nice to see that nothing's changed about this place. I ought to stop by Freedom Fudge Factory and see if they still make their Eggnog Fudge. I haven't been able to find anything like it elsewhere. You wouldn't happen to know if they do?"

"They do, as well as the Peppermint Chocolate Fudge you like. But that's beside the point. You're trying to dodge my question."

He winced. Josephine could still read him like a book. Nothing got past her inquisitive eyes and ears. He tried to make light of the situation with a cheeky grin. "That's because there's nothing to fret about. I'll have you know the rig's medic gave me a clean bill of health."

"Aren't *you* the rig's medic?"

"I am. That's why I trust my own medical expertise."

"Jack," she drawled, sorely unimpressed with his sense of humor, "that's not funny. You shouldn't joke about this. Health isn't something you can take for granted. You might feel great one day, but the next day you're having—never mind." Arms crossed, she turned toward the passenger window, signaling the end of their conversation.

Jack blew out a long breath. Apparently, their walk down memory lane had to include the unpleasant parts, too. Not one to engage in confrontation of any kind, Josephine used to let her silence speak for her. It seemed not much had changed. He didn't feel like arguing either, so he opted to keep quiet as well.

Thankfully, they soon turned into Josephine's apartment complex, so Jack switched his attention to finding a parking spot. The three-story building called Freedom Lofts looked inviting with large windows and a small balcony for each unit. Light shone from behind many of the drawn curtains. He pulled into an open space near one of the staircases and turned off the engine. They sat in silence for a good minute before Josephine faced him.

With her face partially hidden by the shadows, she murmured, "I'm sorry. I shouldn't have gotten so upset. I think this health scare has me on edge."

Jack's heart softened. Having Josephine try to reconnect with him was such an unexpected blessing. "No, you were right. I shouldn't have made light of the situation. But really, I'm fine. I had my annual physical done last month—by a licensed doctor, I might add. I'm as healthy as can be for my age."

"What about your heart?"

His heart? It was in desperate need of forgiveness from his ex-wife, but now wasn't the right time to tell Josephine that. He simply replied, "It's good. No more heart palpitations, I promise."

"What about your cholesterol and blood sugar levels?"

"Within normal range."

"Really?"

"On the higher end of normal," he admitted, "but still normal."

"Blood pressure?"

"All good."

"Do you get regular colonoscopies and prostate screenings?"

Even though this felt like an interrogation, he couldn't help but grin. This had to be a sure sign that Josephine still cared about him. "Yes and yes."

"Good."

"Anything else you'd like to ask, Nurse Gilbert?"

"That's all for now," she answered with a satisfied lilt to

her tone. "I'm glad you've been taking care of yourself, Jack."

"I try. I do what I can and leave the rest up to God."

"Well, that's all anyone can do."

"Thank you for your concern, Josephine. It means a lot to me that you still care."

"Of course, I care. I never stopped—" She cleared her throat and faced forward. A light dusting of snow covered the windshield that she stared at intently. "What I mean is that you're the father of my children. I know how worried Jeremiah and Jess were about me this week. I wouldn't want you to be ill in any way and have them be worried about you, too. That's all I meant."

For a second, Jack was tempted to turn on the car's interior light to see if Josephine was blushing. It was a telltale sign of hers when she was embarrassed. Not that he wanted to out her like that, but it would be good to know how she really felt about this situation—about *him*. He needed to know if there could be any reason for him to hope for more with Josephine.

The awkward silence between them was cut short when Josephine cracked open her door. A gust of icy cold wind blew inside the vehicle. "I should get upstairs. Thank you for the ride, Jack."

Jack's jaw dropped as he watched Josephine slowly swing her feet out to the snowy ground. "Hold your horses! What do you think you're doing?"

"Going to my apartment," she replied over her shoulder. The scarf covering her head fluttered in the wind. "Would you bring me my walker, please? And if you wouldn't mind carrying my bag up for me, that would help a lot. I don't think I can manage it and the stairs at the same time."

"You can't possibly be thinking about going up the stairs with a walker! Do you know how dangerous that is?"

"I'm not using the walker *on* the stairs, just to get to

them."

"And then what?"

"Then I'll need you to bring the walker up for me, too."

"Hold on a sec. I can't talk to you like this." Jack humphed, frustrated by the fact that he was staring at the back of Josephine's head. He got out of the driver's seat and rounded the back of the car until he reached her side. Pulling the door open wider, he asked, "Now, how do you plan on going up the stairs without your walker?"

She raised her chin to look him in the eyes, a challenging glint lighting up her baby blues. "Sideways."

"Come again?"

"I'm going to face the railing, hold onto it, and go up one step at a time. Like a crab."

"Last time I checked, crabs don't climb stairs."

"If they did, that's how they'd do it."

Jack ran a hand through his hair, grabbing at the ends in frustration. He couldn't believe how stubborn she was being about this. "And where did you learn this method?"

"I watched a video."

"You watched a video? You and I both know you learn best by doing."

"Not all the time."

"Most of the time. Remember how we watched hours of baby care videos before the twins were born, but you didn't feel confident about changing their diapers until you actually did it yourself? You didn't even like practicing on a doll. So, until you've learned how to do this crab walk in physical therapy and have had plenty of chances to practice it, you're not going anywhere near the stairs by yourself."

Her face flushed, despite the cold temperature. "Then how do you expect me to get to my apartment?"

"Like this." He reached into the car and scooped her up in one swift motion. "I'm carrying you."

9

*J*osephine yelped in surprise. The last place she ever expected to be was in Jack's arms again. "I don't need to be carried!" she protested loudly. "I'm a grown woman, for crying out loud! I can walk up a flight of stairs."

"I know you're strong and capable, but that doesn't mean you need to do everything yourself." He gave her a dubious look. "You don't always have to be the helper, Josephine. It's okay to receive help once in a while."

"But I—oh!" A gasp replaced the rest of her sentence as Jack tightened his hold. When he ambled toward the staircase, she had no choice but to stop struggling. The steps could get icy at times, and she didn't want to make it difficult for Jack. She reluctantly clasped her hands behind his neck and murmured, "Fine. Thank you."

"Thank *you*. Now let's get you out of the cold."

A flurry of snowflakes suddenly blew off an awning and fell upon them, causing Josephine to duck her head. The next thing she knew, she had her face buried in the crook of Jack's neck. It was such an instinctive reaction; she didn't think twice about the consequences until she inhaled. His familiar scent hit her like a tidal wave, enveloping her in long-lost memories. Of the nights when he had carried her just like this to their room after the kids had gone to bed. The intimate way he used to hold her that made her stomach dip and her cheeks flush. And the tender look in his eyes that had told her she was the most important woman in his life.

Until the day she wasn't.

That sobering thought jerked her from her trip down memory lane. Josephine pulled away from Jack and focused instead on taking her keys from her coat pocket. She made it a point to avoid his eyes, even though she felt him watching her. Her fingers clutched the cold metal while the rest of her body heated up under his gaze. Why was this taking so long? She desperately needed some distance from her ex-husband. Each second spent being this close to him felt like a stab to her vulnerable heart.

By the time they entered her apartment, she was ready to leap from his arms. Unfortunately, in her current condition, she remained at his mercy. She could only bite her lower lip and wait as he took his time stomping his wet boots on the doormat before entering. Once he had flipped on the light, she quickly pointed to the forest-green loveseat across the room. "You can put me down there."

"Sure."

If she didn't know better, Josephine would think Jack was the one having trouble walking. His steps slowed like he was underwater, fighting against a strong current. She lifted her chin to meet his gaze and instantly regretted doing so. There was a longing in his eyes that made the past and future collide. Her heart yearned for what it had once known and also wondered what could be, but her mind knew it wasn't possible. No, she had to be seeing things. Either that, or Jack was also caught up in the nostalgia that this moment brought up. After everything they'd been through, there was no way he desired anything romantic with her.

Did he?

Jack finally set her down against the cushions. He removed her sneakers, then pulled a throw blanket from the back of the couch over her lap. "How's that? Are you comfortable?"

"Yes." Josephine winced at the breathy rasp in her voice. She really needed to pull herself together and stop reading into things. "I'm good. Thank you again for your help, Jack. I appreciate it, even if it doesn't always seem like I do," she added with a wry smile.

"I know," he replied with a good-natured chuckle. "I should thank you, too. It's nice to know this old body of mine can still carry you up a flight of stairs without any problems. It's been a while since I carried anyone."

"You mean you don't carry any of the women you date?" Josephine cringed. The question had flown out of her mouth before she could stop it. Now she sounded like a jealous ex-wife, which she so did not want to be. "Don't answer that, I was joking. Um, do you mind turning up the heat a little? The thermostat's down the hall."

"Sure. You still like it set at seventy-two?"

She blinked, surprised he remembered this small detail. "Yes, that'll be fine."

The moment Jack stepped away, Josephine could breathe freely again. As strange as it was to be alone with him in her apartment, she was thankful to be home. She'd only lived in this place for two weeks and still had much to unpack. Her gaze flitted around the room, eyeing the stacks of boxes taking up space on the tan-colored carpet. Normally, seeing such a mess would grate on her nerves, but she was too tired to mind. What she really wanted to do was change into her flannel pajamas and read the latest Marcus Warner adventure thriller. All she needed was for Jack to bring her things up and, more importantly, to leave her be.

She couldn't risk having any more slipups in his presence. She'd said too much already when she'd practically interrogated him about his health. Of course, she still cared about her ex-husband, but he didn't need to know that. In fact, the less he knew about how she felt or what she thought, the better. Having Jack back in Freedom only complicated things. At her age, she had neither time nor energy for complicated matters of the heart.

"I turned the heat up, Josephine," Jack remarked as he walked back into the living room. He wore the same black coat from the other day, but this time paired with jeans and a dark red sweater that complemented his complexion. "You've got a nice place here. I hope you don't mind that I checked it out. I wanted to make sure nothing was out of the ordinary since you'd been gone for a week."

"Oh, thank you for doing that, but there's no need to worry. Jan and Pete came by yesterday to drop off food. And my next-door neighbors are very friendly and overly curious, for lack of a better word. I'm sure they would have called me if anything had been amiss."

Jack nodded. "It's better to be more careful than not, what with you living on your own."

"I appreciate your concern, but it's a safe neighborhood. Jeremiah checked it out for me before I moved in. And I've been on my own for a while now. I know how to take care of myself."

"Right." A pained look crossed his face before he broke off eye contact. "I'll go get your stuff from the car." He strode toward the door, then turned around. "Can I borrow your house key? I want to lock the door."

Josephine quirked a brow. "You're just going downstairs, Jack."

"I'd feel better knowing you were safe."

"I *am* safe. Nothing's going to happen to me in the few minutes that you're gone."

"Josephine, humor me, please."

There was nothing humorous about the deep lines etched between his brows. She knew Jack had grown up in some sketchy places as a child, but this reaction was certainly over the top. Still, it wasn't anything worth arguing over. She placed her keys in his outstretched palm, careful not to let their fingers touch. They'd had enough contact for one day. "Here you go."

"Thank you." Jack smiled. "I'll be right back."

Once he had left the apartment, Josephine's phone rang. To her delight, she saw Jan's name flash across the screen. "Hi, Jan, I'm so glad you called."

"How're you feeling, friend? Are you all settled in at home?"

"I'm good, all things considered. I wouldn't say I'm settled in just yet. Jack's bringing my things up from the car. Once I have my walker, I'll feel less like an invalid."

"Hold on, did you say Jack? I thought Jeremiah was picking you up."

"He was, but plans changed." Josephine explained the situation to Jan, only to have her friend murmur something indiscernible on the other end of the line. "Did you say something, Jan?"

"Don't mind me. I was talking to the Lord."

The playful lilt in her voice made Josephine curious. "About what exactly?"

"Just about some hopes and dreams of mine."

Uh-oh, she recognized that tone. "Jan, don't you go getting any ideas in your head. Nothing is going on between Jack and me. That ship sailed a long time ago—quite literally —when he left to go work on that rig."

"But he came back to Freedom. He came back for *you*, Jo. That ought to count for something."

"It's a nice gesture on his part, yes, but it doesn't mean anything. His life is on the other side of the world. And honestly, he could have any woman he wants. You should've seen these two nurses at the hospital falling over themselves just to be near him. One even had the gall to ask him for his number."

"Did he give it to her?"

"Nope," she replied, a little too smugly. She cleared her throat. "Not that it would have mattered if he had."

"Hm-hmm. I've known you long enough to know when you're not telling the truth. And you are clearly lying to one person right now—*yourself*—because I'm not buying any of this."

Josephine picked at a loose thread on her blanket and sighed. "Why can't you let me be, Jan? I just had brain surgery. I'm not ready to deal with the past or the feelings I get when I'm around Jack."

"So, you still have feelings for him! Tell me more."

"There's not much to tell. I never stopped caring about him. He was my first love. They say you never forget your first love. I'm afraid whoever 'they' are, they're right." She placed a hand on her chest. It felt like her body couldn't catch a break. Not only was her head sore, so was her heart. "It would be so much easier if he hadn't come back."

"I know. But easier isn't always better. Think of it this way—this is an opportunity that God has given you and Jack. Don't waste this gift, Jo."

She balked at Jan's words but held her tongue. She'd

always been too headstrong for her own good, she knew that. Plus, she believed Jan meant well. Her friend had gone through a lot in her own life and had gained wisdom through those experiences. But the way she talked made the situation seem so straightforward when it was anything but. Josephine did however appreciate the reminder Jan had given her, of how she'd prayed for an opportunity to make amends with Jack. This could be her chance.

"Maybe you're right, Jan."

"Come again? I want to make sure I heard you."

"I said *maybe* you're right," she replied with a smirk. "I agree that there must be a reason Jack and I are in the same place again after all these years. Maybe it's time we finally got closure about the past. I'm going to have to pray long and hard about this."

"I'm glad to hear that, Jo. I know it's not as simple as I make it sound, but perhaps it's not as complicated as you think either. I'll be praying for you both. In the meantime, you two can share the oatmeal raisin cookies I left for you. I remember Jack had a sweet tooth. I'm sure a little sugar could help get the conversation rolling."

"You brought me oatmeal raisin cookies? Bless you, Jan!"

"With mini chocolate chips, too, just the way you like them."

"You're the best. Thank you for all your help. As soon as I'm feeling better, I'm going to take you and Pete out for dinner."

"Great! Maybe we can make it a double date."

"Jan!"

Jan laughed. "You can't fault me for wanting to see my friends happy!"

Josephine groaned, ready to give Jan a piece of her mind, when she heard the sound of keys jingling outside. "He's back! I'll talk to you later!"

She composed herself just in time before the front door opened. But one look at Jack's grim expression made her heart drop. "What's wrong?"

"Someone drove off with my rental car and took everything in it!"

10

_J_ack couldn't believe he'd forgotten to close the passenger door of his rental car. From the moment he'd picked up Josephine, he'd been laser focused on keeping her safe in his arms. He'd also been so consumed by memories of their past that he couldn't think straight. So, he'd practically handed the vehicle over to the thief. Now whoever had driven off with the midsize sedan also had Josephine's bag and walker. So much for being helpful. He'd only made the situation messier.

At least the police had come on the scene in a matter of minutes. That was one of the benefits of having an officer for a son-in-law. Duncan and his partner Ty had been patrolling Main Street just a mile away when Jack put in the call. They had rushed right over to the apartment building and gotten busy interviewing the residents on the first floor that Jack had already talked to before they arrived. Unfortunately, no one had seen or heard anything out of the ordinary. All they had to go on were a trail of footprints left in the snow beside where the car had once been parked.

Now Duncan had come up to Josephine's apartment to gather more information.

"Is there anything of value in your bag, Mom?" he asked as he stood beside the couch where Josephine lay. His wide shoulders filled out the black jacket he wore over his police uniform. "Any jewelry? If there's something that the thief could sell at a pawn shop, we could get a lead on the individual that way."

"No, no jewelry. I knew I wouldn't be able to wear any during the surgery, so I didn't bring any with me."

Despite her calm answer, Josephine appeared unsettled. Ever since Jack had told her about the theft, her complexion had paled. He wondered if she was simply worn out from the hospital stay, but it seemed like there was something she wasn't saying. It was times like this when he wished he could read her mind. That skill would've made life a lot easier and possibly even saved their marriage.

Their communication had been the first thing that had broken down when he'd started working overseas. Distance wasn't the issue now though; it was trust, or lack of it. But Jack was more than ready to listen to Josephine. If only she were willing to talk.

"What about a wallet, Josephine?" Jack inquired as he sat down in the recliner near her feet. "Did you have your wallet in your bag?"

"Yes, but there wasn't any cash in it. Just my driver's license and a few credit cards. I'll cancel them."

"Yes, you should do that as soon as possible." Duncan closed the small notepad in his hand and returned it to his pocket. "At least you didn't lose anything important."

Josephine frowned. "Well... never mind."

"If there's something you need, Mom, I can go buy you a replacement," Duncan offered. "It's not a problem at all."

"What is it?" Jack pressed her gently. "Did you have a

favorite shirt packed in your bag? Or a book? I'm sure we can get you another of whatever is missing."

"It's my Bible, the one my Grammy gave me, and also a journal. Those things can't really be replaced." She released a long breath. "It's okay. Let's hope that whoever took the car will be blessed by the Bible and that he won't bother to read my ramblings."

Jack swallowed hard. He knew how much those two items meant to Josephine. Her grandmother had been the one constant in her life when her parents had been too busy working to care for her. And her journal writing had been a favorite pastime of hers for as long as he could remember. Losing them probably felt like losing parts of her past and herself. He couldn't help but feel guilty for her sadness. "I'm really sorry about this, Josephine. I take full responsibility for what happened."

"Why? It's not your fault, Jack."

"It is when I was the one who left the car door open. I can't believe I did that."

"You did?" Josephine burst out with a laugh. "I guess I'm not the only forgetful one today."

"But you had brain surgery. Me? I have no excuse."

"Well, you did have your hands full."

"That's true," he agreed with a smile. For a split second, his and Josephine's gazes locked like they used to when they shared an inside joke. The connection was so strong and sure, he wished he could capture the moment in a photograph and look back on it. But it was over before he could blink.

Duncan spoke up, ready to tackle business again. "At this point, our best shot is contacting the rental company to find out if there's a GPS tracker on the vehicle. I'll get on that right away. Hopefully we can locate the car and get you your things back, Mom."

"Thank you, sweetheart. I appreciate your help."

"Of course. I'm glad to see you doing better. And I'm sorry this happened to you guys. Thank God both of you are safe; that's what matters the most."

"Yes, definitely." Jack nodded. "Keep us posted, will you?"

"I will. You guys have a good night." Duncan began walking toward the door but turned around after a few steps. His thick brows drew together as he glanced at Jack, then at Josephine and back again. "Are you going back to the Lodge tonight, Dad? Or are you planning on staying here?"

Jack blinked and ran a hand along the stubble on his jawline. Duncan's question was so unexpected, it completely threw him for a loop. "I—uh, why do you ask?"

"I was going to offer you a ride since you don't have a car at the moment," Duncan continued, "unless you're going to stay and help Mom—"

"He can take my car," Josephine cut in. "I'm obviously not going anywhere, Jack. You're free to use my car until you can get another one from the rental company."

Jack held his hand up in protest. If he didn't know better, he'd think Josephine was in a hurry to get rid of him. But now that he'd had a moment to think, he realized what needed to be done. "I appreciate the offer, but I think I should stick around tonight."

"Whatever for? If you think the person who took your car's going to come back here, I'm sure they have better things to do. Isn't the first rule of thieving 'never go back to the scene of a crime'?"

Duncan's hazel eyes lit up in amusement. "It's actually the opposite. The saying goes, 'a criminal *always* returns to the scene of a crime.'"

"Oh. Well, sayings aside, I'll be fine. There's no need for you to stay, Jack. I've taken up enough of your time as it is."

"Actually, there is a need," Jack retorted in a firm tone.

"Since you don't have a walker now, you'll need someone to help you around. I'm more than happy to be that person."

"That's right!" Duncan exclaimed with an eager nod. "Good thinking, Dad."

Josephine balked, not seeming at all fazed by the circumstances. "I'm sure I can get another walker from the hospital tonight. Let me give them a call."

Jack and Duncan stood by, waiting patiently as Josephine contacted her doctor. Based on the way her expression changed over the course of the call, Jack assumed the conversation wasn't going as she'd hoped.

She confirmed as much when she hung up a few minutes later. "I can't believe this. In order for me to get a new walker, the insurance company needs the doctor to place the order. But that can't happen tonight because he's already gone home for the day. All I could do was leave a message."

There was no denying the disappointment in her voice. Jack wondered if she just wanted to be left alone or if she specifically didn't want *him* around. He thought of an alternative. "Would you rather stay at Jess and Duncan's tonight? Would that work, Duncan?"

"Of course. You're more than welcome to come over, Mom," Duncan piped up. "Jess already came up with a plan in case you wanted to stay with us. She got you a bell to ring to call us whenever you need anything. It'll be like having your own personal room service."

"If Josephine doesn't take you up on the offer, I just might," Jack joked. "That sounds really nice."

"That does sound nice, but..." Josephine chewed on her bottom lip, a sign Jack recognized as her weighing her options. A planner by nature, she'd always been more cautious than him. This trait, as with any, was both a strength and a weakness. She made her decisions wisely but took longer doing so. After a pause, she continued, "I think it's more convenient if I stay here tonight... with Jack."

Both Jack and Duncan cocked their heads in surprise.

"You want me to stay here tonight," Jack asked for clarification, "at your apartment, with you?"

"If you don't mind. Practically speaking, it makes sense. Duncan has to work late, so if I stayed with them, it would be Jess helping me around the house, which would not be safe for her or the baby. But you're physically strong enough to help me around and even catch me should I, God forbid, lose my balance. This is the right thing to do for everyone involved."

"That does make a lot of sense." Jack couldn't agree more, but he tamped down his enthusiasm. He needed to tread carefully. It was a positive step that Josephine was accepting his help, even if it was for practicality's sake. He hoped it was a sign that she was starting to trust him again.

"I think that's a wise choice, Mom." Duncan flashed her a thumbs-up. "I know Jess will sleep a lot better knowing that Dad is here with you. I'll be off then. Good night!"

Duncan let himself out before either of them could say a word. The door closed with a loud thud, leaving Jack and Josephine to stare at each other in awkward silence. Jack wiped his damp hands along his jeans, feeling like the tenth grader who was about to ask the girl of his dreams to the movies. At least that instance with Josephine so many years ago had ended on a positive note. He had no idea, however, what would become of tonight.

11

*S*mall talk—Josephine had a love/hate relationship with it. That's what she and Jack had filled the silence with after Duncan had left. Five minutes was all she'd been able to stomach before she suggested they eat dinner. She appreciated being able to chat about things like the weather when the time was right, but too much mundane talk made her uncomfortable. Especially when it involved someone she knew better than anyone else. Or someone she used to know well. The man moving about in her kitchen had Jack's mannerisms and voice, but she wondered if he was truly the same person she'd once been married to.

Did he still like putting ketchup on everything?

Was he still accustomed to drinking a cup of coffee every night after dinner?

Could he still fall asleep as soon as his head hit the pillow even after downing all that caffeine?

"Do you have any ketchup, Josephine?" Jack asked as he stuck his head back into the living room where she was lying on the couch. His brows furrowed in disappointment. "I didn't see any in the fridge or in the cabinets."

She bit back a smile to have her first question answered. "It's in one of the boxes over by the wall here. The one marked with a K. I hadn't gotten a chance to unpack it yet. I spent a lot of the past two weeks at Jess's."

He strode over and unstacked a couple of boxes until he found the right one. Meanwhile, Josephine's breath caught in her throat as she observed every one of his familiar movements. The way he bent at his knees to carry something heavy—a habit he'd gotten into after throwing out his back swinging the kids around when they were small. How he pushed the sleeves of his sweater up to his elbows before digging into the box. And the sight of his forearm muscles rippling as he held up a bottle of ketchup like a trophy.

"Found it!" His face lit up, giving him a youthful appearance. "Now we can eat!"

Josephine couldn't help smiling. She'd always loved that about Jack, how even small things could bring him such joy. "I've never known anyone else who loves ketchup as much as you do. Maybe you should start carrying around a bottle with you wherever you go."

"Great idea." He regarded her with a thoughtful smile. "I always did like the way you think. Remember how the twins used to play with their train set early in the morning and the sounds would wake us up? You came up with the idea to put tape over the speakers. I thought that was brilliant."

She shrugged off his compliment. "It was just me being practical."

"Well, I always loved your practical side. It got us out of plenty of binds back in the day."

"Thanks." Josephine pursed her lips, not knowing how else to respond. To hear Jack mention loving any part of her felt so right, yet so wrong. Was this how exes normally talked? Things had certainly changed since the last time they saw each other. It was a sure sign that God had healed both of them over time. But this new level of communication felt a little too comfortable. It'd been a lot easier for her to dislike Jack than to feel whatever emotions were stirring in her heart.

Switching to a safer topic, she asked, "Is the casserole almost done?"

Ding!

"There it is," he announced as the oven timer went off. "Let me set the table and we can eat."

Josephine released a sigh of relief as Jack walked away. Getting along with him like this reminded her too much of the past and made her miss those days... and maybe even miss *him*. She needed to focus. Focus on what she needed to accomplish, which was to clear the air about their past. This was the perfect opportunity to do so. And after tonight they could go their separate ways again.

Just one night, Lord. Please help me get through it in one piece.

In a matter of minutes, Jack was at her side. "Would you like me to carry you to the table?"

"I can walk just fine, thank you. But if you wouldn't mind helping me up..."

"Of course not." He extended his hand to her. "Easy now."

Taking his hand, Josephine rose from the couch, then stood with the bulk of her weight on her right foot. Jack's arm immediately came up around her shoulders to support her. The act served to keep her from falling, but it made her stomach dip in a dangerous way. They were close again, so awfully close.

Now is not the time to be thinking about how good Jack smells, she chided herself. The faster she moved, the sooner she'd have some space from him. She forced herself to take a step forward.

"I've got you," Jack assured her. "Just lean on me."

Josephine gritted her teeth. That was easy for him to say!

He wasn't the one fighting the urge to bury her face in his sweater so she could inhale his familiar scent. It also didn't help that each one of her wobbly steps pushed her closer to him. Her upper body was now completely flush against Jack's with one arm clutching his waist for balance.

It would only take a single turn of her head to come nose to nose with him. The thought alone made her cheeks burn. This wasn't such a good idea after all. Who knew how long it would take for her to limp to the dining table? "You know what, I changed my mind. It would be a lot faster if you carried me. At the rate I'm moving, Jan's casserole will be cold by the time we make it over there."

Jack chuckled softly and scooped her up. "Sure thing."

Just as she predicted, Jack had her seated at the small round table in two seconds flat. He took the chair across from hers and began dishing up their food. Savory hints of bacon, eggs, and cheese wafted in the air, bringing a contented smile to her face. What a blessing to have dinner prepared for her. And the company to share it with wasn't half bad either.

Who was she kidding? Being able to spend time with Jack was like a dream come true. It was the re-do she'd once longed to have. In those lonely days and months following their divorce when the kids had moved out of the house, this was what she'd wished for—a simple meal with him. Maybe if they'd been able to freeze time and be on the same side of the world for once, they could have recaptured what they had lost. She'd always believed that if he'd stuck around Freedom, their marriage could have stood a chance.

It was too late now for such wishful thinking.

"Want to say grace, or should I?" Jack's question broke through her musing.

"Why don't you?"

"Sure." He bowed his head and prayed, "Lord, we thank

you for bringing Josephine through her surgery safe and sound. We ask for Your healing hand to be upon her as she recovers. Thank you also for this time we can spend together and for the good food before us. In Jesus's name, amen."

"Amen." Josephine took an extra moment to enjoy the sense of peace that washed over her. When she opened her eyes, she found Jack squirting ketchup over his helping of breakfast casserole. He looked like an artist at work, adding color to his masterpiece in elaborate swirls. She couldn't get over the fact that while Jack had aged on the outside, he was still the same boy she had fallen for. A lump grew in her throat thinking of the good times from their past. The dates they'd gone on as teenagers when the best part of the evening was getting to hold each other's hand. And the tender nights they'd shared as a married couple when they'd done so much more.

What had happened? How had their relationship come to this point? They had vowed to grow old together, not apart. Yet, here they were, broken and beyond repair. If only she could rewind time and try again. If she'd been more patient and understanding, would things have turned out differently?

"You're not eating," Jack remarked when he looked up from his plate. "Do you need help with anything?"

"No, I'm fine. Just taking my time." She picked up her fork and took a small bite. "This is delicious. Jan outdid herself."

"She sure did. I'll have to go over and thank her. It's been ages since I saw Pete, too. I can't believe the two of them tied the knot. How're they doing?"

"They're good. Busy with two grandkids now." She released a long breath. "It's crazy, isn't it, knowing we're all grandparents now? It doesn't seem like that long ago when we were all in high school together."

"My back would disagree," he joked. "It feels every one of those forty years that have passed since graduation. Did you happen to attend the reunion last year? I thought about coming back, but my schedule wouldn't allow for it."

"Mine either. I was in the middle of expanding my clinic at the time. I heard from Jan that they had a good turnout."

Jack offered her a pleased smile. "I'm really glad you got to live out your dream in California. You always wanted to have your own midwifery practice, and you made it happen. It couldn't have been easy."

The lump returned to her throat, making it hard to swallow or speak. If he only knew how many times she'd almost given up. Starting life over in a new state had been the scariest thing she'd ever done. She took a long sip of water before answering, "It wasn't easy, but God pulled me through."

"I'm thankful for that. I'm thankful He kept you safe all these years, Josephine. I often wondered how you were doing."

She eyed him cautiously. "You did?"

"Of course. Even though we weren't together anymore, I still cared about you."

She waited for him to add a disclaimer, such as "because you're the mother of my children," but none came. Then again, Jack had always loved people unconditionally. His heart was pure in a childlike way. She'd never had to second-guess his intentions before, why was she doing so now?

"It probably wasn't obvious based on the way I acted at times," he continued with a pained expression. "I'll be the first to admit that my behavior at Jess's wedding wasn't very mature. I want to apologize to you for that."

Clang!

Josephine was so surprised; she nearly dropped her water as she set it down on the table. It hit the edge of her bowl before Jack righted it. "Thank you. For catching the glass, not for the apology."

"You don't accept my apology?"

"No, I don't mean that. The thing is, *I'm* the one who should be apologizing to *you*. I was quite rude to you and your date that night. I still feel bad about the horrible things I said. I'm sorry."

"I appreciate the apology, but you really didn't say anything wrong. In fact, what you said woke me up to the fact that I *was* having a midlife crisis. It's the tough love I needed to hear."

"You're being much too nice, Jack. If you only knew half the things I didn't say out loud that I'd wanted to say, you wouldn't feel this way."

"Ha!" The corners of his eyes crinkled as he laughed. "Thank God you held back then. I don't think I could have handled any more. It was hard enough seeing you that day and knowing that you were doing so well on your own. Not that I wanted you to be doing poorly—"

"I get it," she cut in. "You don't have to explain. I felt the same way."

"Yeah?"

She took a deep breath. If Jack could be so transparent with her, she could do the same. "I'd never been so conflicted between wanting to see you suffer and wanting to see you succeed. It was enough to give me whiplash with how much I flip-flopped. But ultimately, at the end of the day, I was glad you were okay... even if that meant you were okay without me."

His lips curved into a bittersweet smile. "That's what I wanted you to think."

Josephine's heart stuttered in her chest. What did Jack mean by that?

---

12

*T*he shocked look on Josephine's face surprised Jack. How in the world could she believe he'd been better off without her?

"Were you not okay, Jack?" she asked, her tone hesitant. "Have you not been okay all these years?"

He set his fork down, having lost his appetite. Regret sat like a boulder in his stomach as he considered everything he wanted to say. Was this the right time? How much was too much? He prayed for wisdom and patience to speak the truth. "I haven't been okay in a long time. I've been getting by, but have I been happy? Quite frankly, no. My life hasn't been the same without you. *I* haven't been the same without you."

Josephine stopped chewing. She stared at her plate for a while, her lips pursed. When she finally lifted her gaze to meet his, she murmured, "I understand the loneliness. Going from being part of a couple for so many years to being single took a while to adjust to. It helped that I had my work to keep me busy. Didn't you as well?"

"It wasn't just loneliness, Josephine; it was more than

that. I lost my sense of purpose. I had a job to keep me busy, but I didn't have a reason to work so hard anymore. You and the kids had always been the driving force behind why I did what I did. I thought you knew that. That's why I took the oil rig job because it gave us more stability and we were able to give the kids everything they needed."

So they wouldn't have had to grow up like I had, he wanted to add. Jack, however, knew that Josephine didn't understand the pain of going without. It wasn't for lack of trying though. She'd sympathized with him when she'd learned of his struggles, but she'd never experienced being hungry or cold. Her parents had always given her the best of everything. That's why he'd strived so hard to provide her with that same level of comfort.

Apparently, everything he'd done had still not been enough.

"I know you worked hard to provide for us, Jack, but what the kids needed was you, not fancy sports equipment or brand-name clothes. I don't know why you could never understand that. We just wanted you home. You didn't have to go halfway around the world to provide for us."

"I wasn't making nearly enough at the time. Don't you remember how we had to scrimp and save up every single penny to pay for braces? We couldn't even get the kids Christmas presents that year."

"They didn't mind that at all. The only thing they asked for was to go to the tree lighting ceremony and the parade with you, and that's what we did. They were so happy you were able to get time off from work. That's what mattered, spending time together as a family." Her voice reflected the weariness in her slouched shoulders. "All the presents in the world could never take the place of that."

Jack opened his mouth to reply but closed it again. At that

moment, he realized he had nothing helpful to say. The points Josephine had brought up just now were the same as twenty years ago. Nothing had changed. She had always wanted more time together, while he had focused on the practical aspects. Neither side was necessarily right or wrong. They each had different needs they wanted to address. The problem was that they both thought their need was more important than the other person's, and there was no use stating otherwise. Jack had tried time and time again to no avail. He'd spouted off every logical reason he could think of decades ago to which Josephine had responded with her own list of objections. Their arguments had gone back and forth until they withdrew to their own corners, angry and divided.

He didn't want to be divided anymore.

Everyone should be quick to listen, slow to speak, and slow to become angry.

The verse from James 1:19 popped into Jack's mind, cutting through his frustration like a beam of light. When was the last time he'd listened to Josephine? Really listened to her instead of just biting his tongue before he could speak his piece. Had he ever tried?

Jack ran a hand down his face, then blew out a long breath. It wouldn't hurt to try.

"I want to understand your side better, Josephine. Can you tell me more?"

Her brows furrowed as she stared at him across the table. The sound of the kitchen faucet dripping filled the silence. She eyed him with what could only be described as suspicion. "What do you mean, Jack? I don't understand what you want me to tell you. We've been through this before and it never got anywhere. I'm feeling pretty tired. I think I should turn in—"

"Josephine, please." He winced, knowing he'd already lost

the fight by interrupting her. "Sorry, I shouldn't have cut you off."

"It's fine."

"No, it's not. I used to cut you off a lot, and it wasn't right." He held his hands up in a gesture of peace. "I'm realizing now that I don't think I ever really listened to you before."

She gave a quick shrug. "What's past is past. It won't help to talk about it now. Let's just move on."

"I'm trying here, Josephine. I want to listen to you now. Will you give me a chance?"

"I appreciate the thought, Jack, but I don't have anything left to say that I haven't said before. And I'm exhausted. I just want to sleep in my own bed and get a good night's rest."

Jack nodded. The dark circles under her eyes told him she wasn't making excuses. This wasn't the time to press her to talk. "All right. Let me help you."

"Thank you."

He lifted her gently from her chair and cradled her to his chest. A smile crossed his lips as he breathed in the floral scent of her perfume. Having grown up in a family of three boys, he'd never appreciated how much better the opposite sex smelled until he met Josephine. It was like that old nursery rhyme equating girls to sugar and spice and everything nice. She was sweet and spicy and everything in between. The feeling of holding her felt both new and as old as time. He'd lost count of how often he'd carried her when they were married, but he'd never get tired of it. And he would treasure every opportunity he had during his time here to carry her.

"Can you bring me to the bathroom first?" Josephine asked as she looked straight ahead. She held herself still in his arms like a statue, but her cheeks were more flushed than any inanimate object could ever be. Clearing her throat, she added, "I'll need a couple of minutes to get ready."

"Sure thing." He flipped on a light switch, illuminating a short, bare hallway. It was so unlike the home he and Josephine had made for themselves in Freedom where nearly every wall had been decorated with framed photos of the twins along with their annual family Christmas pictures. He wondered if she'd be putting them up here and, more specifically, if he'd be in any of them. "Do you plan on hanging up any pictures? I can help put them up for you."

"I haven't thought about it yet, but thanks for offering."

"No problem. Feel free to let me know if you change your mind." Jack walked past two open doors on their right until they reached the bathroom at the end of the hall. "I also noticed the kitchen sink's got a leak. I'll have a look at that later."

She turned to face him, her brows raised in surprise. "You don't have to do that, Jack. I didn't ask you to come here to be a handyman."

"I don't mind. I'm here, so you might as well put me to work," he joked. "I won't have anything to do while you're sleeping."

"I'm sure you can find something. There are books in one of the boxes in the living room. Or you can use the computer and watch those history documentaries you love." She paused. "Unless you don't watch them anymore?"

"I do. You remember that about me?"

"How could I not? That's all we ever had playing on the TV, even during our honeymoon. If I ever have a chance to go on Jeopardy, I'm sure I'd have no problems acing their World War Two questions."

Jack laughed in delight. He appreciated these unexpected moments of reminiscing. "You can thank me later if you ever do. However, if I remember the honeymoon correctly, we were too preoccupied with other activities to do much watching."

The color in her cheeks darkened as she caught on to his unspoken message. "I-I wasn't thinking about that. You can put me down now, Jack. Please."

He was about to set Josephine on her feet when the hallway light flickered. They both turned to look at the fixture on the ceiling.

"Looks like the bulb needs changing," Jack remarked. "I'll have a look at it."

"It's not a big deal. It probably just needs to be screwed in more—"

The light went out completely.

"Tightly," Josephine finished in a droll tone. "Or maybe it needs a new bulb like you said."

"I couldn't have planned that better if I'd tried. That was good timing, wasn't it?"

"You got lucky," she agreed with a soft chuckle.

Their shared laughter filled the hallway that now seemed smaller, thanks to the darkness enveloping them. He couldn't make out Josephine's features, but he felt her warm breath upon his skin. His heart pounded in his chest to be this close to the only woman he'd ever loved.

Time seemed to slow down while memories from their past rushed to the forefront of his mind. Dancing at prom. Late night study sessions during college. Getting married at the courthouse, then taking a road trip across the state for their honeymoon. The birth of their children. And celebrating each and every milestone after that as a family.

Marrying Josephine had been the best decision he'd ever made. And their marriage of twenty years had been the best years of his life. What they'd had was good, so good. Yes, they had messed up badly before, but they were both older and wiser now. Why couldn't they capture that goodness again?

That's when he realized Josephine was wrong. He was more than lucky; he was blessed. Blessed beyond belief to have this second chance.

Lord, thank You for Your mercy and grace. Please help me to make the most of this opportunity.

As their laughter died down, the mood shifted from playful to calm. Neither moved nor said a word, yet the quietness of the moment spoke volumes. The chemistry between them had not changed; if anything, it was stronger than ever. An invisible cord pulled Jack closer to Josephine until his forehead touched hers. She gasped softly, making him wonder what it would feel like to kiss her again.

"The, uh, bathroom light!" Josephine suddenly exclaimed as she pulled back. "We can turn that one on."

It took a few seconds for her words to register. "Oh, right." Jack quickly reached past the doorframe and flipped the switch on with his elbow. They both blinked as their eyes adjusted to the brightness of the vanity light.

Josephine avoided his gaze as she murmured, "Thank you for your help, Jack. I'll let you know when I'm done."

Disappointment twisted his gut. What had happened? Gone was the intense connection from a second ago. In its wake was an uncomfortable silence that reminded him too much of the final days of their marriage.

Patience, a still, small voice spoke to his heart. *Give her time.*

Jack heeded the advice and carefully let Josephine down, steadying her until she was stable on her feet. Then he stepped away while she closed the door, leaving him in the dark in more ways than one.

13

A new day with a clean slate—that's what Josephine hoped for when she woke up the next morning.

Snuggling under her comforter, she savored a few more moments of rest. Her apartment heater, as old as it was, had kept her room nice and toasty. With no one waking her up every few hours to check her vitals, she'd slept better last night than she'd had in days. Her head still ached a bit from where she'd had the surgery, but overall, she felt much stronger and more alert. And now that she was well rested, she hoped she'd be better able to tackle whatever obstacles came her way today.

Because she had a feeling there would be more of them.

Who would have believed that she'd spend the night in the same apartment as her ex-husband? Surely not her. But as she'd learned over the years, some surprises could be unexpected blessings. So, she'd trusted in God's all-knowing wisdom and providence when she'd accepted Jack's offer to stay. The talk they'd had at dinner, while brief, had given her so much relief and reassurance. Being able to apologize to him and hear his apology in return had been a true gift. It did her heart good to know that they had moved past the bitterness and anger of the past. She thanked the Lord so much for that.

But then...

She shook her head in wonder. What had happened—or nearly happened—afterwards with Jack still had her stomach tied up in knots.

You're not a teenager anymore, Josephine Gilbert, she chided herself. *There's no room for emotions or wishful thinking.*

It was time to wake up, figuratively and literally. She took a deep breath and forced her eyes open. Without her glasses, she couldn't see the clock on her bedside table clearly, but the sunlight streaming in through the curtains indicated it was already past seven. The light cast a warm glow on the carpet, its color reminding her of the Rice Krispies treats she had made with her grandkids recently.

Had it only been a week and a half ago?

It felt like so much had happened since then. She wasn't thinking only of her brain aneurysm and the subsequent surgery. The more pressing matter at hand was the fact that she had almost kissed Jack last night!

She placed a hand over her mouth, feeling her warm breath beneath her fingertips. She'd kissed Jack enough times in the dark before to know exactly how it would have played out ... if she'd given in. One inch more, and she would've felt his lips on hers; there was no doubt about it. What she doubted though was knowing how she'd ever come back from a kiss like that. Because in her heart of hearts, she could no longer deny the truth.

She was still in love with Jack Gilbert.

The urge to kiss him hadn't been due to the darkness or their close proximity, although those things had certainly helped. What had driven her to even consider it was his sincerity, plain and simple. His apology had been so heartfelt and honest. Then when he'd offered to listen to her, really listen, she'd felt the wall around her heart crack in two.

This was the boy she'd fallen for when she was fourteen. Catching glimpses of him made her yearn again for the might-have-beens and even believe that they could come true.

But they couldn't.

She and Jack had no future together. He would be going back to the other side of the world soon, while she would be staying here in Freedom. It was the same old story, just a different time. If she'd learned anything from experience, it was to not put her hope in temporary things. Instead, she pushed her longings aside and focused on the first obstacle of the day—getting out of bed.

"Come on, you can do it," she murmured to herself as she threw off her comforter.

Next, she reached for the glasses she'd set on her night table and put them on. The room came into focus, as did her determination. If she had to hop to the bathroom, so be it. She needed to do whatever it took to regain her independence. With or without a walker, she didn't want to be at the mercy of her children or Jack to get around. Where there was a will there was a way, and she'd figure it out.

A moment later, Josephine had managed to push herself to a standing position by the side of the bed. Her face was probably the same color as her pink pajama top from the physical exertion, but she felt pretty proud of herself. With the left side of her body still weak, she kept the bulk of her weight on her right foot. Now she just had to take it nice and slow and shuffle her way to the door.

Josephine had only taken two steps when something in her line of sight caused her heart to lurch. Sticking out near the foot of her bed were a pair of large feet—Jack's feet! What in the world was he doing on the floor?

She hobbled over to him as fast as she could, holding onto the edge of the bed for support. As soon as the rest of his body came into view, her breath caught in her throat. He lay on his back, eyes closed, his face expressionless. "J-Jack?"

When he didn't respond, she fell to her knees and placed her hands on his torso. She ran her palms along his cotton T-shirt, feeling for any sign of movement. To her relief, his broad chest began rising and falling beneath her fingers. Still needing more reassurance, she leaned in close and craned her ear to his nose. A second passed before a puff of warm air caressed her cheek, then another. She'd never been happier to hear his soft snores. She held still, soaking in the comfort that each breath gave her, along with his familiar musk.

Oh, thank You, Lord! She sent a heartfelt prayer of gratitude heavenward. *Thank You for keeping Jack safe!*

Tears burned her eyes as a lump formed in her throat. All her worries from the past two decades came rushing back, full force. There hadn't been a day when she hadn't thought of Jack or wondered how he was faring. When they'd been married, she'd always feared for his safety and well-being on the oil rig. Those fears hadn't stopped when they'd gotten divorced, but the reassurances that he was okay had. She hadn't realized until this very moment how much worry for Jack she'd been carrying in her heart.

"Hey," Jack's deep voice murmured in her ear as one of his large hands covered hers. "What's going on here?"

Josephine turned to face him. "You're awake!"

"I am." His amber eyes blinked away sleep as they focused on her. "But if this is a dream, I don't mind sleeping some more."

The smile on his handsome face made her stomach flutter. How was it possible for her to react the same way to him after all these years? She supposed her body had grown older, but her heart was still the same, still captivated by Jack's charm and sweet nature. It surprised and scared her to be affected this way. She sat back, needing to put some distance between them. "I'm sorry I woke you up."

"Don't be. This has got to be my favorite wake-up call ever. I do have one question though. What were you doing just now?"

"I was—it was nothing." She cleared her throat as she pulled her hand out from under his. The last thing she wanted was for Jack to know how upset she'd been over him. But his raised brows told her he already suspected something was up. "If you must know, I saw you lying on the floor, and I thought you were hurt. I was making sure you were still breathing."

His eyes never left her face as he raised himself to a sitting position. "You were really worried, weren't you?"

Having Jack validate her feelings unlocked the dam of tears she had stored up. A single drop fell down her cheek, followed by another. She lowered her head and quickly wiped them away. "It's this health scare. It has me overreacting about everything."

"Hey, it's okay." Before she could protest, Jack drew her into his arms and rubbed her back. "I'm fine, Josephine. I'm alive and well."

"I know, but why were you sleeping on the floor?" she cried into his shoulder. "Why didn't you sleep in the guest room like you were supposed to?"

"I wanted to stay close in case you needed me in the middle of the night. I was afraid I wouldn't be able to hear you from the other room. You know I can sleep deeply sometimes."

"Sometimes? Try all the time! You didn't even hear me calling you from a foot away."

"I'm sorry. I didn't mean to worry you."

Josephine fought to catch her breath. She couldn't believe how badly she'd overreacted. Jack had always been a deep sleeper, so much so that he'd never heard the twins' cries in the middle of the night when they were babies. She should have remembered that about him instead of letting her emotions get the best of her. Here she was doing the complete opposite of what she wanted. But being near him felt so good and right. She'd missed the strength and security of his embrace.

Just a few more minutes, she reasoned with herself, *and I'll pull away. I don't know if I'll ever get to be this close to him again.*

The years, along with their pain and sadness, fell away moment by moment. After a while her tears stopped, leaving her eyes swollen and her throat raw. It'd been so long since she'd cried in front of another person. Jack had been the only one she could ever let her guard down around.

He had held her just like this each time her parents left her alone at home during her teenage years. He'd been the first person she'd run to after her grandmother had passed. When her parents were too busy to attend her college graduation, Jack had been the one to take her to her favorite restaurant to celebrate. Through every hill and valley in her life, he had been her one constant, a tangible reminder of God's grace in her life and that she was never alone.

After the divorce, she did her best to stay strong for the kids. Then work took over her life, allowing her to hide her true emotions with busyness and activities. She knew it'd only be a matter of time before she wouldn't be able to hold them back anymore. But she never thought she'd do so in his arms.

This is temporary, Josephine. Don't get used to it, she reminded herself. *The sooner you let go, the less it will hurt.*

It was time to face reality. She steeled her heart and pulled away. With a bittersweet smile, she patted the large wet spot on Jack's chest. "I'm sorry about your shirt. You should change it before you catch cold."

His eyes met hers, darkening with intensity as they flicked to her mouth and up again. Taking her hands, he brought them to his lips and placed a lingering kiss on them. "I don't care about the shirt. I care about you. I want another chance, Josephine. Please, let's try again."

14

"*J*ack, we can't."

He shook his head, unwilling to accept those three words from Josephine's lips. What did she mean? There was nothing standing in their way of getting back together. They had overcome the hostility of the past and forgiven one another. The way she had allowed him to hold her as she cried spoke more loudly than the answer she gave. "Why not? I still love you. You're the only woman I've ever loved. We've missed out on so much when we were apart; I don't want to miss out anymore. I want to grow old with you."

She scoffed softly. "We're already old, if you haven't noticed."

"*Older* then," he quipped back. "I'm talking about the kind of old where we'll be cleaning our dentures together and the highlight of our day will be going shopping for batteries for our hearing aids. I want to experience all of that with you."

"You forgot to mention playing Bingo at the senior center."

"We can certainly do that, too."

Josephine's blue eyes sparkled with amusement, but she shook her head. "I know how sincere you're being about this, Jack, and I appreciate your intentions, but it's not that simple. Your life is on the oil rig and I'm here in Freedom now. Our circumstances haven't changed at all. We're still in two different places, which was the same issue we had before."

A spark of hope came to life in his chest. Josephine hadn't said no, which he took to be a step in the right direction. "So, you're saying that distance is the only thing keeping you from saying yes?"

She pressed her lips together, deep in thought. When she spoke, her tone was gentle but firm. "It's okay, Jack, you don't have to try so hard. We already went our separate ways a long time ago and we've built two very different lives since then. The kids are all grown with their own families now and they're both doing well. You don't need to feel responsible for us anymore."

"Responsible? I'm not saying these things out of obligation. Is that what you think this is about?"

"I know it wasn't all out of obligation. We certainly didn't get married out of obligation. But having to provide for a family—that put so much pressure on you. You said it yourself, Jack, that we were the reason you worked so hard. We were the reason you had so much stress. Don't you remember? You used to toss and turn in your sleep every night and you barely had time to eat. You were constantly popping antacids and taking migraine meds. I can still picture how tired you always looked." She paused to glance down at her hands. "I never wanted a divorce. Giving you that ultimatum was the most foolish thing I've ever done, but maybe it wasn't wrong to set you free. You no longer had to carry that burden that weighed you down so much."

He shook his head, not believing what he was hearing.

"That's not what I meant at all! Yes, I took it as my responsibility to earn money for our family, but it wasn't a burden. I *wanted* to provide for you and the kids; that's why I worked so hard. I didn't want us to end up like my parents—living paycheck to paycheck and having to choose whether we paid rent or bought food each month. That's not how I wanted *my* family to live."

"I know, Jack. I know you wanted to do it your way, and I respect that. But—" Releasing a deep breath, she continued, "Never mind. This is all in the past. It's pointless to talk about it now."

Jack opened his mouth to protest further, but the ringing of his cell phone cut him off. "It's not pointless. We obviously have some things we still need to discuss. Hold your thought. We're not done with this conversation yet."

Josephine's only response was a quick shrug of her shoulders.

He picked up his phone from the spot where he had set it next to his makeshift bed last night. "Hello?"

"Good morning, Dad, it's Duncan," his son-in-law greeted him. "I've got some good news for you."

"Hold on a second for me, will you?" Jack couldn't believe his eyes. In the span of a few seconds that he'd taken his eyes off Josephine, she'd gotten up from the carpet and was now hobbling over to the door. He stuffed his phone into his pocket and rushed over to her. "I'm here to help you. Why do you insist on struggling on your own?"

"This is nothing, Jack, I've been through worse," she huffed out as she allowed him to place an arm around her shoulders. With his support, they made it to the bathroom. She turned to give him a small smile. "I appreciate your help, but I'm going to have to do this on my own sooner or later. I'd rather it be sooner, so I can help Jess when the baby comes. You go on and take your call. There's no need to wait for me."

He stared in awe at the back of her head as she shut the door behind her. Josephine never ceased to amaze him, in both good ways and bad. No one expected her to be up and running only a week after having brain surgery, least of all their children. He'd have to find some way to convince Josephine to slow down. For now, he took a deep breath and returned to his phone call.

"Thanks for waiting, Duncan. What's the news?"

"We located your rental car. It was found in an alley across town. Looks like some kids took it for a joyride, then left it there. The rental company's going to have it towed back to their lot. They said you can pick up a new vehicle from them whenever you like."

"That *is* good news. I'm glad you found the car. What about Josephine's bag?"

"I have it with me right now. I can drop it off on our way home from church if that's okay. Jess and Titus would like to see you guys, too. Is Mom up for a visit?"

"She'd run a marathon right now if she could," he answered, only half-jokingly. Josephine was still as determined and stubborn as ever. He wouldn't put it past her to try. "I'm sure she'd love a visit."

"Great. We'll see you soon."

After Josephine finished her morning routine, Jack helped her to the dining table where they ate breakfast mostly in silence. Jack had a feeling she was done with their conversation from earlier and decided to drop the subject. One thing he'd learned from the twins when they were young was to never discuss important matters on an empty stomach. He prayed for patience and wisdom to know when and how to broach the topic of reconciliation again. Perhaps what Josephine said was true—things weren't as simple as he'd thought. They still had matters from the past to hash out. There had to be a way to move on, so they could consider the possibility of a future together.

"Do you want to watch the sermon online?" Josephine asked when they finished eating.

"Sure. I could use some teaching from the Scriptures right now."

Josephine looked at him curiously as she started up her laptop. They spent the next hour watching Freedom Bible Church's live-streamed worship service, sitting side by side on the couch. It reminded Jack of their early days of dating when they'd rent a movie from Blockbuster and spend the evening holding hands over a bowl of popcorn. What fond times those had been. He still remembered that regardless of whether they were hanging out at Josephine's huge house or at his small, leaky one, she hadn't seemed to care. As long as they were together, she was happy.

Could it be that he was the only one who had minded?

Jack found himself dwelling on this question as he listened to the sermon, a sermon that seemed to be tailor made for him. He'd heard many pastors share from the book of John before, but the way Pastor Stephenson preached made the verses come to life for him.

Then Jesus declared, "I am the bread of life. Whoever comes to me will never go hungry, and whoever believes in me will never be thirsty." (John 6:35, NIV)

For Jack, the concept of literal hunger was not new. He'd experienced it over and over again when he was young, and the fear of going without was what drove him to make money. He felt secure and happy when his bank account was full. With each passing year, he'd been able to save up more and more, to the point that he had the most money now than he'd ever had in his life, yet he still felt the need to work. He was still hungry. How much would ever be enough?

"What are you thinking about?" Josephine asked as she closed her laptop and set it aside. "You're so lost in thought, you didn't even notice the service ended."

Jack met her gaze with a sheepish smile. "I was thinking about how I'm always hungry."

Concern creased her forehead. "Did you not have enough to eat at breakfast?"

"No, I meant figuratively. It's hard for me to be content with what I have. Even with all the money I've saved up over the years, I feel like it's not enough. How do you do it? You never seemed to worry about money like I did."

Understanding lit up her eyes. "Of course, you worried more; you were the only one working to support the family. You had more pressure on your shoulders, pressure that I couldn't share."

"But I don't have that pressure anymore. Yet, I still feel like I can't stop working. I wish I could be as satisfied as you always were."

"It's not a fair comparison to make, Jack. We grew up so differently. I had more than enough material things in my life. I guess, in the back of my mind, I always knew I could ask my parents for help if I needed it. I didn't need money to feel secure." She paused, chewing her lower lip. "Despite what you think of me, Jack, I'm not that different from you. I have things I hunger for, too; they're just different from yours. But that's the beauty of what Pastor Stephenson talked about. That in Jesus we don't have to hunger anymore. He can meet all our deepest needs when we ask Him."

Jack looked at Josephine, really looked at her. He sensed there was so much that she was holding back on telling him. How was it that she understood him so well, yet he felt like he didn't know her at all? "What is it that you hunger for?"

She grew quiet for a moment. Just when Jack wondered if

she would ever answer, she said softly, "I suppose the main thing was companionship, knowing that I wasn't alone in the world. That's what I hungered for before. But God has been so faithful to meet my needs. I don't feel alone anymore."

Jack swallowed hard. Suddenly, it dawned on him what he had failed to see this entire time. His decision to work abroad had put Josephine in her most vulnerable state. She'd been left on her own to raise their children. He'd done the very thing that her parents had done—abandoned her emotionally. His own insecurity and fears had blinded him to what she had so desperately needed. He may have been a good provider, but he'd lacked in every other way.

I messed up, Lord. I see that now. How do I make things right?

More than anything, Jack wanted to make it up to Josephine for all the ways he'd disappointed and hurt her in the past. Maybe she didn't need him the same way that she once had, but he still longed to be a part of her life. To support her, encourage her, and to walk through all the highs and lows by her side. He prayed that she would allow him this privilege.

Jack reached for her hand and clasped it in his. When their gazes locked, he asked, "What about now? Do you still want companionship? Do you want companionship with *me*?"

15

Josephine's heart hammered in her chest. She'd tried to avoid this topic earlier, but here was Jack bringing it up again. She didn't fault him for being persistent; she just wished she were stronger. Her heart was so soft and vulnerable. A single glance, touch, or smile from Jack, and she felt forty years younger. Oh, to be nineteen again and so innocent and oblivious to the troubles that lay ahead. But knowing what she knew now, she would still have chosen to marry Jack and raise a family with him. He was the best friend she'd ever had. Of course, she still wanted companionship with him. How could she say no to the only man she had ever loved?

"Of course, I do," she admitted before she could stop herself. "But I also don't."

"What do you mean? You do or you don't. There's no in-between."

"There kind of is. It's like when the kids were learning how to swim and Jess was too scared to get in the water. She saw how much fun Jeremiah was having and she wanted to try it, too, but she just wasn't ready." She glanced down at their intertwined hands resting on the couch cushion between them, her heart heavy with regret. What she didn't say was how this analogy only explained half her story. The reality was that she'd already jumped into the water before and had nearly drowned. She and Jack had failed once already. What would prevent them from failing again? "I'm not ready, Jack."

"I understand your hesitation, but think of how much fun you'll have once you're in the water. There's nothing to fear, Josephine. You won't be alone. You'll have me. I'll come back to Freedom for good to be with you." His voice carried so much hope and tenderness as he promised, "I won't let you sink."

"You would give up your job for me?"

"In a heartbeat." He turned to face her fully. "I'm not talking about retiring yet—God willing, I think this old body of mine can handle a few more years of work—but I can find a job here in town."

"As what? A paramedic?"

"Sure. That's what I'm trained in, so it makes the most sense. It'll take some time for me to get used to working in a box again," he remarked, using the nickname for *ambulance*, "but I'm sure it'll be like riding a bike. It's all muscle memory."

"Jack, you don't know how to ride a bike. I was the one who taught the twins how to ride."

He chuckled. "I know. I meant it as a metaphor."

The twinkle in his eyes made her laugh, too. Josephine shook her head in wonder. The Lord had sure worked in both of their hearts these past twenty years. What Jack was offering sounded too good to be true. To have him come back home to Freedom to be with her—without any nagging or pleading on her part—was what she'd longed for. But the last thing she wanted was for him to return to work as a medic.

"What if I said you didn't have to work? That you could retire and spend your days doing a much more important job?"

"What job is that?"

"The role of Grandpa."

He grinned. "That has got to be my favorite job so far. I would love to do that instead of work, but someone has to pay the bills. I would rather be the one working so you can spend time with the grandkids."

"I can do that already. It's you I'm talking about. I can't bear the thought of you working those long hours again. Don't take this the wrong way, Jack, but you're not as young as you used to be. You've worked so hard all these years; it's about time you took a break. I have enough money saved up. More than enough for the both of us," she added with a hopeful smile.

His jaw grew slack with surprise. "Both of us? Does this mean you're ready to take the leap? You're ready to jump into the water together?"

Was she ready? Josephine inhaled deeply as she felt Jack's large, warm hand caress hers. A peace filled her from within, giving her the courage to nod. "I'm ready."

Jack's entire countenance brightened. The corners of his eyes crinkled as his eyes shone with unshed tears. He pulled her into his arms and gently kissed the top of her head. "Thank you, Josephine. Thank you for giving me another chance. And thank the Lord for giving us both this chance."

"Thank you for taking this jump with me." She leaned into his embrace, letting her tears fall freely. Tears that came from a place of relief and happiness and hope. It was amazing how God had used something as unpredictable and scary as her aneurysm to bring about this reconciliation. He truly did work all things together for good.

She pulled back to meet Jack's gaze. Her breath hitched in her throat as she cupped his face and looked him full in the face. This was the first time she allowed her gaze to linger as she took in all his features. She smoothed the lines between his brows that had grown deeper with time. The stubble along his jawline, now filled with gray, tickled her fingertips. His lips, the only lips she'd ever kissed, parted in a kind smile.

"Are you wondering who this old man is that you're looking at?"

"You may be older, but you're more handsome than ever. It's been so long since I've had a proper look at you, I don't want to stop. I've missed being able to see you and touch you."

"Is there anything else you've missed? What about kissing me?"

A flutter awakened in Josephine's stomach, making her blush. "That, too. Have you missed kissing me?"

"You have no idea." He tipped her chin up, his gaze dropping to her mouth. His voice grew husky with desire as he asked, "May I?"

"Please."

Josephine closed her eyes, expecting to feel Jack's lips on hers. Instead, he kissed her on the forehead first, then on her cheeks. The warmth of each touch sent a thrill through her body. When his mouth finally found hers, she could no longer hold back. She placed a hand on his chest, feeling the beating of his heart beneath her palm, and clutched the cotton fabric of his shirt. Pulling him closer, she deepened the kiss and showed him just how much she had missed him.

There was no need to second-guess and no more room for regrets. She was all in, without reservations and without any doubt. God knew her heart's desires and had provided for her once again. She would not take this chance for granted. Jack was home, and he was here to stay. And she would love him so much better this time around.

Her heart was so full when they pulled apart. Now there was so much more to look forward to in retirement. Not only would she get to spend time with her family, but she would be doing so with Jack. She couldn't wait to start making plans with him.

"This is going to be so much fun, Jack. The grandkids are going to be so excited to spend time with you. Miah's been talking about going sledding and Asher and Adam want to build a snow T. rex—they're in a whole dinosaur phase right now. I promised them and Titus that we'd make gingerbread houses together. We can have a sleepover with all the kids and build blanket forts like we did when the twins were small. And when the new baby arrives, there will be one more little one to love." She sighed happily. "Retired life is the best, Jack, you'll see. Being around the little ones really keeps you young and active. There won't be any time to be bored. But if we ever want adult conversation, we can always meet up with Jan and Pete for a game of cards."

"That all sounds great. It also sounds a lot more tiring than working. I might need a retirement plan for my retirement plan," he joked. "I can't wait to spend time with the grandkids. I haven't spent nearly enough time with them. And I'm looking forward to spending time with you." Jack raised her hand to his mouth for a kiss. "I didn't expect to be retiring so soon, but I have no complaints. Thank you, Josephine, for making this possible."

"Please call me Joey. *Josephine* just doesn't sound right coming from you."

"Yes, ma'am." The smile on his face said it all. He pulled her close and wrapped his arm around her shoulder. "I still remember the first time I heard your grandmother call you Joey and how you said I could call you that, too. I felt like the luckiest guy in the world. Everyone else at school called you Josephine, but I got to call you Joey."

She snuggled into his side, feeling more content than she had in a long while. "That's because you weren't like everyone else. You were my best friend. You *are* my best friend. I've missed you so much, Jack. I wish we hadn't waited so long to reconnect. We lost so many good years together."

"I know. I feel the same. But we have all the time in the world now to spend together. It'll be like reliving our youth, without the struggles and cares we had back then. Knowing we don't have to worry about money takes a lot of the pressure off. You're amazing, Joey. How did you manage to save up so much?"

"I sold my practice and the house I had in California. The cost of living is so much lower in Colorado, so what I made from those sales will go a long way here. Add to that my inheritance money and there's more than enough to live off of."

"Your inheritance money?"

"Yes, from my parents." She gazed up at him. "By the way, I never thanked you for the flowers you sent me when they passed away. That was really thoughtful of you."

Knock, knock, knock!

The soft sound coming from the front door interrupted their conversation.

"That sounds like Titus knocking," Josephine remarked with a laugh. "He tries so hard, but his little hand can only do so much."

"He'll get there eventually." Jack pulled away and stood up. "I'll get the door."

Josephine couldn't stop herself from beaming with

excitement. She could imagine how thrilled Jess would be to hear that her parents were back together. The rest of the family would no doubt rejoice with them, too. For the first time in a long time, she looked forward to Christmas. Not only would they be celebrating Christ's birth, but also the rebirth of her and Jack's relationship.

She hoped and prayed there would be no obstacles standing in their way from here on out.

---

16

*J*ack couldn't believe how much had changed over a day. Just yesterday, he and Josephine had agreed to rekindle their relationship, and today, they were behaving like a couple of newlyweds. Between the stolen glances Josephine shot him from across the physical therapy room and the encouraging thumbs-ups he gave her in return, there was hardly a minute when they didn't make eye contact. These interactions reminded him of their early days of dating when emotions ran high and hormones even higher. They might not be young anymore, but this relationship certainly felt new. He thanked the Lord over and over again to have been given this second chance.

"Good afternoon, sir." A young woman dressed in blue scrubs approached Jack with a smile. Her name tag read *Michele*. She handed him a small stack of paperwork and sat down beside him in one of the chairs lined up against the wall. "I'll give these to you to hold onto for your wife. It's a summary of the exercises and routines she's learning today that you can practice at home."

"Thank you." Jack paused, wondering how to clarify his

and Josephine's relationship. "She's actually my ex-wife, but we just made up. We're giving our relationship another shot."

"Oh, that's wonderful! I don't think I've ever heard of anyone getting back together after a divorce." Her brown eyes lit up with curiosity as she glanced at Josephine who was using an exercise band with the help of her therapist. "What happened, if you don't mind me asking?"

He chuckled. "What didn't happen is the better question. We've been through so much, the two of us. We hadn't talked or seen each other in years when a health scare brought us back together last week."

"I'm sorry that happened."

"Me, too. It's unfortunate that it took a brain aneurysm to bring us to our senses, but I'm grateful God took something bad and turned it into something good."

"He's really good at doing that, isn't He?"

Jack nodded wholeheartedly. "The best."

He followed her gaze as she looked around the room at a couple of the other patients who were in the middle of their sessions. One older gentleman was practicing going up and down a ramp while another rode on a stationary bike. A middle-aged woman walked up a short flight of stairs that Josephine had used earlier.

Turning back to face Jack, Michele remarked, "Your story just reminded me of what the Lord did for this hospital after the fire."

"There was a fire here?"

"It happened eight, nine years ago. You don't know about it? It was on the front page of the Freedom Gazette for months. I'm guessing you're not from around here?"

"I grew up in Freedom, but I hadn't been back in a while. Was it a bad fire?"

"There was quite some damage, but thankfully, no one

was seriously hurt. But what came out of it was almost too good to be true. A couple donated enough money to rebuild what was damaged *and* open up a couple of new wings, one of which was this outpatient physical therapy wing. It was like Christmas morning when we had the ribbon cutting ceremony after everything was built."

Jack's eyes widened. "Sounds like it was a big donation."

"Very big," she agreed, "and just what this town needed. Now our patients don't have to travel to Denver to get the same type of rehabilitation. We have all the best equipment and staff right here. And we have the Waltons to thank for that."

Jack's stomach clenched. "Did you say the Waltons?"

"Yes, why? Do you know them?"

"I did," he uttered, his throat dry, "a long time ago."

While he hadn't heard that surname in years, it had been on his mind ever since yesterday's conversation with Josephine. He still remembered her words clearly.

Add to that my inheritance money and there's more than enough to live off of.

That one line had thrown him for a loop. Of course, Josephine's parents would leave their money to her, their only child. But for her to insist on using her inheritance to support their retirement—Jack hadn't expected that at all.

Even now, he couldn't shake how much Josephine's parents' disapproval had affected him. Hearing their name transported him to the first time they'd met. He'd shown up for dinner in his best clothes, but they were no match for Mr. and Mrs. Walton's diamonds and pearls. All they saw was a poor boy who they believed only wanted to date their daughter for her money. That was the assumption he'd worked so hard to prove wrong. Yet he would soon be indirectly relying on the very people who had once scorned him.

The irony was not lost on him one bit. He would be lying

if he said the situation didn't hurt his pride. But was this something worth agonizing about?

"Are you okay, sir?" Michele's soft voice drew him back to the conversation. She placed one hand on his arm and gave it a gentle squeeze. "Were you thinking about the Waltons? I heard they passed away in an accident a couple of years ago. I didn't mean to bring up any sad memories for you."

"No, it's fine," Jack reassured her. "You didn't say anything wrong. I did know them, but we weren't exactly friends."

"Well, friends or not, I'm sure if they were still alive, they'd be happy to know your ex-wife, or girlfriend rather, is benefitting from their contribution."

Jack cracked a smile. That much was certainly true. "You're right. I know they would be happy. Josephine meant a lot to them."

Michele nodded enthusiastically as she rose to her feet. "It was nice chatting with you, but I better get back to work. If you or Josephine have any questions about the handouts, let me know."

"I will, thank you."

Jack turned his attention to the paperwork, intending to familiarize himself with the exercises so he could help Josephine practice them at home. His mind, however, couldn't focus. An uneasiness stirred inside his heart, making his body restless. Thinking about his former in-laws often did that to him.

He decided to head to the cafeteria to grab a snack for Josephine. She was working so hard during this first session of physical therapy and would no doubt be hungry afterwards. He soon felt a burden lift from his shoulders. Focusing on someone else's needs always gave him a sense of purpose. By the time he was in line to pay for a protein bar and a bottle of water, he had a small smile on his face.

Instead of dwelling on the past, he really ought to be planning for the future—his and Josephine's future. God had done a miracle in bringing them back together. What he needed to do now was think about how and when he could start transitioning his life off the oil rig. There was so much to do, from giving notice at work, to packing up and moving his belongings, and finding a place to stay here in Freedom.

Was it too soon to bring up the topic of marriage with Josephine? Would she expect him to propose again? What would rebuilding a relationship that had been through the wringer look like? He had more questions than answers, but one thing he was certain of was the love he and Josephine had for each other. Everything else, they would figure out in time.

"Mr. Gilbert! Fancy seeing you here!"

Jack turned around to see the familiar face of a young woman he'd met at Freedom Ridge Lodge last week. His daughter-in-law Haven who worked as the event planner there had introduced him to the friendly and talkative physician assistant. "It's good to see you, Casey. How are you?"

"I'm doing great. Just grabbing some caffeine before my shift starts. The coffee here's not nearly as good as what Mountain Mug serves, but it does its job. You wouldn't believe how busy it gets around the holidays in the Cardiology department. The other PAs and I joke that all those family gatherings must be responsible for an increase in high blood pressure and chest pain."

He smirked. "That's probably not far from the truth."

She frowned, producing a line across her forehead. "I hope that's not the reason why you're here."

"No, not at all. I'm waiting for my ex-wife; she's in the

middle of a physical therapy session." He moved ahead to the register and paid for his items. "This snack is for her."

Her blue eyes widened. "You two must be on good terms. I've never heard of a divorced couple being this civil with each other."

Receiving this kind of comment a second time made Jack's smile widen. "All I can say is that God still does miracles. We're being more than civil; we've started dating again."

"That's amazing! It's so rare for people to give each other a second chance."

"That's unfortunately all too true," Jack replied with a sigh. The Waltons once again came to mind. At least his former in-laws had not let their prejudice against him influence how they had treated their grandchildren. They had showered Jess and Jeremiah with plenty of toys when they were young, toys Jack hadn't been able to afford. Now that he thought about it, he wondered if those expensive gifts had been a subtle jab at him? Perhaps he was assuming too much. He pushed his concerns to the back of his mind as he stepped out of the line.

Casey gestured for him to wait as she paid for her cup of coffee, then followed Jack out into the brightly lit hallway. "I'll walk with you. The PT wing's on the way to Cardiology. I'd love to meet your other half."

A grin curved his lips. Thinking about Josephine immediately lifted his spirits. "You mean my better half. Come on, I'll introduce you to her."

When they arrived at the physical therapy room, Jack was surprised to see Josephine sitting outside the open door. She had one hand on the replacement walker they had picked up earlier, her complexion still rosy from exercising. With a light pink sweatshirt and matching pair of sweatpants on, she looked youthful and relaxed and, most of all, beautiful. His heart rate picked up speed within seconds of seeing her.

Jack rushed to her side. "Sweetheart, you're done already? Here, I got you some water."

"Thank you. I just finished." Josephine's gaze flitted back and forth between Jack and Casey. She offered her hand to Casey and introduced herself. "Hi, I'm Josephine. You are?"

"I'm Casey. It's so nice to meet you! Mr. Gilbert told me all about your story, how you were divorced and now you're back together again." Her voice rang out with enthusiasm as she shook Josephine's hand. "I loved hearing about it. Thanks for giving us single people hope."

Josephine's expression softened. "I'm so glad you're encouraged by our story. We can't take the credit though, God's the one who brought us back together."

"I'm sure that's true, but it still takes a lot of faith on your part, especially when things didn't work out the first time around. You fell off the horse, but you're getting back on again. That takes guts."

Jack nodded. "I appreciate that analogy even though I've never been on a horse before. Josephine, on the other hand, started riding when she was three. She earned several blue ribbons when she was young and even won the Colorado Saddlebred Award when she was twelve."

"That's so cool," Casey exclaimed. "I always wanted to learn how to ride, but my family couldn't afford it. Do you still ride?" She sucked in a sharp breath as her gaze fell to Josephine's walker. "That's not why you're in therapy, is it, because you literally fell off a horse? I shouldn't have said that."

"No, you're fine. That's not why I'm here. I had surgery for a brain aneurysm," Josephine explained, pointing to her loose-fitting gray beanie that hid her scar. "I haven't ridden in years, but it's something I did enjoy doing. If you're ever interested in trying it out, I'd be happy to go with you."

"That's so sweet of you! Maybe I will take you up on the offer if I can find time. My work keeps me pretty busy."

A sympathetic sigh emerged from Josephine's lips. "I understand. I used to work in healthcare, too."

Jack watched in amusement as Casey took a seat beside Josephine and began chatting a mile a minute. There was something about the woman he loved that made people want to open up to her. He supposed that's what had drawn him to her all those years ago. She listened attentively to Casey, even though she had to be exhausted from her therapy session. Jack considered helping Josephine out and cutting the conversation short for her, but his cell phone suddenly buzzed in his coat pocket.

He excused himself and stepped a few feet away. The number flashing across the screen made his chest tighten. Why was work calling him?

17

*J*osephine gathered up what energy she had left and channeled it into listening to Casey. The young woman was so chatty and down-to-earth, she imagined it would be easy to befriend her. No wonder Jack had opened up to her. Josephine breathed easy knowing that their conversation had been an innocent one.

Guilt, however, still had her insides twisted into knots. She chided herself for even entertaining the idea that Jack would give into another woman's advances. She'd allowed her insecurity to take over when Jack and Casey had shown up in the hallway together. It didn't help that she'd already been feeling wary from when the physical therapy assistant had placed her hand on his arm earlier.

Both scenes reminded her all too much of when Jack had brought his younger date to Jess's wedding. She needed to let that memory go though. There was no use holding onto the past. She and Jack were in a different place now, a better one. He was back in Freedom for good. She had to trust him and trust in the Lord who had given her this second chance with him.

"So, when are you and Mr. Gilbert getting married again?" Casey's giddy voice broke through Josephine's thoughts. "Because I'd love to come to your wedding! You could have it at the lodge. Haven's so great at planning the events there. I'm sure she could put something together for you in no time at all."

Josephine had to laugh at Casey's enthusiasm. Her new friend was certainly optimistic. "I have no idea. Jack and I just got back together yesterday. We haven't talked about the future in much detail yet. But we will certainly invite you if the day comes. *When* the day comes," she added in her own optimistic tone.

She had a good feeling that there was much to look forward to. Not that she relied on feelings alone, but if she'd learned anything these past two weeks, it was the power of prayer and hope.

Her surgery had been a success.

She'd gotten her grandmother's Bible and her journal back.

She and Jack had reconciled.

It would be the first time in decades that their family would all be together for Christmas.

There was nothing more that she could want. *Thank You, Lord, for making this all possible.*

"I'll be waiting for my invitation!" Casey exclaimed as she stood up. "I gotta run, but it was great meeting you, Josephine. Or should I say Mrs. Gilbert?"

"I haven't been called that in a long while, but it does sound good. It was nice meeting you, too, Casey. I'll be praying for you and your family situation."

"Thanks, I appreciate it!" she called out with a wave.

Jack nodded his goodbye to Casey when she passed him down the hall a moment later. He looked over at Josephine

with an apologetic smile and motioned for her to wait a little longer.

She mouthed, *No problem,* then leaned back in her seat to rest her head against the wall behind her. She'd already waited twenty years for him; what was another couple of minutes? Whatever conversation Jack was having had to be important. The look on his face was both contemplative and serious. He stood tall and straight with the thumb and middle finger of his left hand rubbing his temples. Josephine hoped whoever was on the other end of the line wasn't delivering bad news.

As she sat waiting, her eyelids grew heavier with each passing second. The physical therapy session had really taken its toll on her body. Josephine closed her eyes, intending to rest them for just a few seconds. She only realized she'd dozed off when she woke up with a crick in her neck.

She took a quick glance around the hallway, expecting to see Jack, but he was nowhere to be found. Her stomach dropped. Why would he have left? Did it have something to do with the phone call he'd gotten?

Her thoughts immediately traveled to her kids and grandkids. Had Jess gone into labor already? She quickly found her phone in her purse and checked to see if there were any new messages. The only thing she saw on the screen was the background photo of her four grandchildren. There were no missed calls either.

Overwhelmed with worry, she dialed Jack's number. A phone sounded in the distance, drawing her eyes upward. There was Jack rounding the corner with his phone in hand, heading straight for her.

"Jack!" Josephine was so relieved to see him, her eyes welled up. Leaning on the walker for support, she rose to her feet. "Where did you go? Are you okay? Is the family okay?"

"I'm fine. The family's fine, too, as far as I know. I just went outside to finish my call. I didn't want to disturb your sleep." He cocked his head and studied her face intently. Drawing her into his arms, he murmured against her hair, "What's wrong, Joey? What's got you so upset?"

"I-I don't know. When I didn't see you, I started worrying that something had happened." She released a shaky breath as she hid her face in his chest. "I'm sorry. I don't know why I'm so emotional. I don't usually cry so easily."

"Hey, it's all right. There's no need to apologize. You've been through a lot lately. The surgery alone was stressful enough, but now you're having to relearn how to walk again. You've got to be exhausted. I'd be worried if you weren't emotional." He rubbed her back in soothing circles. "I know you're strong and brave, but you don't have to carry it all on your own anymore. I'm here, Joey. Let me help you. I want to help you."

She nodded, a sob escaping her lips. Jack's words gave her the validation she needed to fully rest in his embrace. She allowed her tears to fall. There was freedom in knowing she no longer needed to hide her feelings from him. She'd done that when they were younger, which had only served to create distance between them, beyond the literal miles that had separated them. Maybe if she'd come clean and admitted how scared she'd been without him and how much she'd needed him, he would have come back home sooner. It was too late to change the past now, but she vowed to change her ways.

Josephine pulled back to meet Jack's gaze. The love she saw in his eyes gave her the courage to confess everything she'd kept from him. "I'm not as strong as you think I am. And I haven't felt brave in a very long time, not since you left to work on the rig. There's so much I should have told you before..."

"What is it?"

"Those two years before we divorced were some of the hardest years of my life. I wanted to be a supportive wife and not worry you when you were working so far away, so I didn't tell you everything that was happening at home. How Jeremiah started acting out and spending time with the wrong kids at school. And Jess, she had panic attacks nearly every day worrying about you. Then there were my parents —they gave me so much grief about you being gone and how you didn't care about me and the kids anymore. I tried to stay strong, Jack, I really did, but it got to the point that I started believing them. I started believing that you didn't want to be with me anymore, that you must have met someone else, and that's why you didn't come home." Regret weighed heavily on her heart when she noticed his eyes fill with tears. "I should have told you everything that was going on then. Maybe it would have made a difference."

"Of course, it would have made a difference," he stated with absolute certainty. "If I had known what was going on with the kids and with you, I would have come home in a heartbeat. I had no idea. I wish you would have told me. Or maybe you did, and I didn't listen?"

She shrugged. "I might have tried a couple of times, but with the time difference, we could never find a good time to talk. Either you were exhausted, or I was. After a while, I guess I stopped trying."

Jack's expression grew somber. He cupped her face and ran the pads of his thumbs across her cheeks. With a gentle touch, he wiped her tears away. His voice broke as he pleaded, "Forgive me, Joey. I never meant to hurt you. I should have been there for you. I should have made sure you and the kids were okay."

Josephine shook her head. "I should have been more honest with you. I should have trusted you and not given in to my fears. In the back of my mind, I'd been afraid that you'd leave me like my parents did. I always felt like they valued their jobs more than they valued me. When you left to work on the rig, it was like my greatest fear had come true. So, I convinced myself that I didn't need you anymore, that I could handle everything on my own. I wish I hadn't pushed you away. I'm so sorry, Jack. Can you forgive—"

Before she could finish her apology, Jack pulled her into his arms. "Say no more, Joey. We've both suffered enough. It's time we moved on from our mistakes. From this point forward, we are going to work together as a team. Let's be open and honest with each other, all right? Don't be afraid to tell me what you need. I will do my best to listen to you. But if you ever find that I'm not listening well enough, I want you to promise to make a doctor's appointment for me because it'll probably mean I need hearing aids."

With her ear pressed to his chest, she heard the rumble of his laughter loud and clear. The happy, familiar sound made her smile. Jack always knew how to make her feel better. She lifted her head and gazed up at him. "I promise to be honest with you. And I'll make that doctor's appointment should the time ever come," she added with a chuckle.

"Good. Now let's get you home so you can get off your feet."

"Not before I show you my crab walk up the stairs. I'm a pro at it now."

"I saw you practicing. That was the most professional crab walk I ever did see." He grinned, then narrowed his eyes. "Are you sure you don't want me to carry you instead? It would be my absolute pleasure."

She pretended to consider his offer before nodding readily. "I think crab-walking can wait."

They shared a laugh as they made their way to the exit. As Jack helped her into his new rental car, Josephine remembered something she'd wanted to ask him. "Who called earlier? You seemed worried when you were on the phone."

"It was nothing much, just a work-related call."

Something in his tone told her there was more that he wasn't saying. The moment he sat down behind the wheel, she placed a hand on his arm. "Jack, I thought we were going to be honest with each other? It sounded like an important call."

His mouth curved into a knowing smile. "You're not going to let me off the hook, are you? You're right, it was important. The headquarters in Texas called my boss and asked if I could cut my leave short. There's a rig in the Gulf of Mexico that needs a medic. Both of theirs got called away, one for a family emergency and one due to shingles, so they're short-staffed. They asked me since I happen to be back in the States at the moment. Everyone else they called already has plans. They know I usually don't mind working during the holidays."

"What happens if there's no medic on board?"

"The rig has to come back to shore until they find a replacement. That could mean days without pay for the staff."

Josephine frowned while she processed this news. As much as she hated the thought of Jack leaving Freedom even for a little while, she knew in her heart what she needed to say. Placing a hand on his arm, she urged him, "I think you should go."

18

---

*J*ack couldn't believe his ears. He'd just listened to Josephine share how much his being away for work had affected her and their marriage, and here she was suggesting that he take on this assignment?

After starting the engine and switching on the heat, he turned to face Josephine. "I'm not going. I already told them I wouldn't be taking the assignment."

"You can tell them you changed your mind," she insisted. "Jack, this is serious. You can't let all those people lose out on their paychecks. They have families to provide for. They're just like us when we were younger, trying to keep their kids clothed and fed. If there's something you can do to make sure they don't lose their income, why shouldn't you do it?"

"I hear what you're saying, but I'm not going to leave you again. Especially not when you're still recovering."

"But I *am* recovering and I'm recovering well. The worst is already behind us. With my new walker and the physical therapy sessions, I'll be back to chasing the grandkids around in no time. You don't have to worry about me. And anyways, this job is only temporary, right? It's not like you're going to be away for months."

"True. It would likely be for a week or two until one of their medics can return from leave."

Josephine gave him an encouraging smile. "See? You could be back by Christmas or New Year's at the latest."

He studied her face, wanting to be sure he wasn't missing anything. "Are you sure, Joey? You're not just saying this because it's the right thing to do?"

"Well, of course I want to do right by these people, but it's not only because of that. I've learned through the years that everything happens for a reason. I believe God planned for you to be back in Freedom and for you to be close to that rig. You need to go and do your part, Jack."

He couldn't deny the wisdom in her words. "I agree. I know there's always more going on behind the coincidences than we see. I still don't feel good about leaving you though. Who's going to help you while I'm away? How will you get to your physical therapy sessions?"

"I found out from my PT that the hospital provides a rideshare service. I just have to sign up."

"Oh yeah? They really thought of everything."

"Rest assured, I'll be fine. I can always call Jan and the kids if I need anything." She reached for his hand. "I'm giving you my support this time, Jack, my full support. I'll be praying for you every day until you return. And God willing, we can restart our life together then."

"You're amazing, Joey. Thank you. I'll be praying for you, too, every chance I get." He placed a lingering kiss on her palm. "When I get back, the first thing we're going to do is talk about the future."

"I'd like that very much."

Jack squeezed her hand, marveling at how well it fit in his. Their fingers were threaded together just like the first time they had held hands as teenagers. Only now, their weathered skin boasted memories of all the hard work they had endured over the years. For him that meant tending to the needs of the sick and injured as a medic and doing what he could do to be involved in their children's lives when they were younger. For Josephine, she'd used her hands to change diapers, wipe noses, feed the family, and make their house a home. Her hands had also been instrumental in bringing countless babies into the world as a midwife.

They each had their own roles over the years and many of their responsibilities had required them to work separately. But now they were doing something together. Sure, he would be the one on the rig, but to have Josephine's full support, as well as her prayers, made all the difference in the world. He could leave Freedom without worry, hesitation, or regret, knowing that Josephine would be waiting for his return.

That's how Jack found himself on an oil rig in the middle of the Gulf of Mexico early the next morning. After ensuring that their kids would check in on Josephine while he was away, he had taken a red-eye flight to Texas. When he landed, he was immediately transported to the vessel where he jumped into work with both feet. From back pain to minor sprains, migraines, and digestive issues—he had seen no less than a dozen patients during his first few hours on board. The remainder of the day was just as busy, as was the rest of the week.

During the few minutes of downtime that he had during work hours, he stayed in touch with Josephine via text. In the evenings after dinner, they chatted on the phone about their respective days. He enjoyed hearing about the progress she made in therapy and all the updates about their grandkids whom Josephine had started to see again for brief visits. The more he heard about everything that was going on in

Freedom, the more eager he felt about heading back home to be with his family.

By the time Friday night rolled around, he was ready to check in with the office about the length of his shift. He finished typing up his patient notes, then placed a call to headquarters.

"Hello Mason, this is Jack Gilbert. How are you?"

"Jack!" the boisterous voice of his superior rang out over the line. "You're just the person I wanted to speak with."

"I'm glad I called then. What's going on?"

"First of all, let me tell you how pleased everyone is with your work. I can't remember the last time I received this much positive feedback in such a short span of time. It's a nice change for once."

"Why, thank you. I'm glad to hear that. Everyone I've met on this rig is great. I've enjoyed working with them."

"That's music to my ears because I have an offer to make you, and I promise to make it worth your while."

Jack's ears perked up. "What do you have in mind?"

"How would you like to stay on longer? One of the regular medics will be coming back tomorrow morning, but the other one is taking an extended leave, so we could really use your help. Having two medics on board will make everyone's lives easier. What do you say?"

"How long did you have in mind?"

"Anywhere from three to six months. I know you've been based out in Angola for a while now, so I thought this change of scenery would be good for you. With you being so close to Colorado, you can easily fly there on the weekends you'll have off."

"I see." Jack leaned back in his office seat and blew out a long breath. This was certainly unexpected. "Being closer to home does sound attractive, but I must be honest, the reason

I called was to give you my notice. I'll be retiring once I'm done filling in over here."

"Jack, no! I'm really sorry to hear that." Disappointment coated Mason's words. "You're one of our best medics. It would be a shame to lose you."

"I appreciate that, but it's about time I retired so I can spend the rest of my days with my family. I'm not getting any younger, you know," he quipped. "I have four, soon to be five, grandkids that I'd like to run around with while my knees and back still allow me to."

"I understand, but you can't fault me for wanting to convince you otherwise. How about this? I'll increase your pay by ten percent if you stay."

Jack's brows shot up. In all his years of working, he'd never been offered a raise so easily. He was tempted to consider it, but Josephine's words came to mind.

This job is only temporary, right? It's not like you're going to be away for months.

He couldn't go back on his promise to her. Returning to Freedom as quickly as possible had to be his number one priority.

Mason must have sensed his hesitation because he quickly countered his offer. "On second thought, make that a fifteen percent increase. I'll throw in a bonus as well."

"A bonus?"

"Yes. Five thousand if you agree to stay six months."

Jack nearly swallowed his tongue. He'd be a fool not to take this offer. "That's very generous of you, thank you."

"So, you accept?"

"I…" He rubbed his jaw as conflicting emotions ran through his body. It would be so easy to say yes, but he couldn't do so with a clean conscience. Would the consequences be worth it?

"Think about all the things you'll be able to do with that

money," Mason continued. "It wouldn't hurt to have some extra saved up for retirement."

Jack couldn't agree more. He would never complain about having more zeroes in his bank account. Having the extra funds would also mean not having to depend on Josephine as much to support them. This bonus was a drop in the bucket compared to her funds, but the less he had to rely on the inheritance money from her parents, the better. He wanted to show her that he could provide for her, too.

"Why don't you take a couple of days to think about it, Jack? Talk it over with your family. I'll be in touch with you next week to get your answer."

"All right," he agreed, heeding Mason's suggestion. It would be wise to discuss this with Josephine before he made a decision. Like he'd told her, they were a team now. And as supportive as she'd been recently, he was sure that if he explained his reasoning to her, she'd agree with him that this was one opportunity they couldn't pass up.

At least he hoped so.

19

"*G*ranny, your walker is the bomb!" Josephine's granddaughter called out the moment she saw her emerge from Jan and Pete's car. Even at age ten, Miah already talked like a teenager. She ran over from where her parents had parked their minivan about ten feet away. Bending down to examine the walker, she ran her fingers along the red and green ribbons that Josephine had tied to the metal handlebars. "I love how you decorated it. Can we take a picture in front of the Christmas tree together later? I wanna show my friends I have the coolest granny in the world!"

"Of course, sweetheart. It would be my pleasure." Josephine wrapped one arm around Miah's shoulders as they hugged. She waved to Jan and Pete who motioned that they were heading to a bench in front of Freedom Fudge Factory.

"Where's Grandad? He didn't come with you?" Miah's green eyes narrowed as she looked around the sidewalk. A small crowd was gathering in the middle of Main Street in preparation for the tree lighting ceremony. She tugged on Josephine's sleeve and frowned. "He said he'd come tonight."

"I'm sorry, Miah. He unfortunately got called away to work. He needed to fill in for someone who got sick."

Miah's shoulders slouched with disappointment under her navy coat. "Will he be back for Christmas? He said he'd take me and Adam and Asher sledding. Did he forget?"

Josephine's chest tightened to see Miah's pained expression. The sadness in her voice reminded her of Jeremiah's and Jess's reactions so long ago whenever Jack couldn't make it home from working on the rig. How ironic. Here she was having the same conversation all these years later with Jeremiah's child. How was it possible that things hadn't changed all that much in two decades? Jack's work still got in the way of family time, and he was still disappointing people.

Even worse, she still had to apologize and make excuses for him.

No, she immediately corrected herself. *It's not the same. Jack promised to come back soon. Have faith in him. He's not the same man he used to be.*

She rubbed Miah's back in comforting circles. "I'm sure Grandad remembers. He's going to try his absolute hardest to come back soon. But the good news is that after he's done with this job, he'll be retiring and staying in Freedom, so there will be plenty of time to go sledding then!"

Her answer seemed to appease Miah who gave her a bright smile. "Cool!"

"What's so cool?" Jeremiah greeted them as he walked up with his twin sons, holding each one by the hand. He gave Josephine a quick kiss on the cheek. "Hey, Mom. I'm glad you could make it tonight."

"What's cool is that Grandad's going to retire," Miah informed him, "and when he does, he's going to move here and stay with Granny!"

Jeremiah's brows shot up. "Who told you that, Miah?"

"Granny did."

"Well, not in those exact words," Josephine clarified with a soft chuckle, "but it's true. Your father and I have been talking about the future, *our* future."

"That's amazing, Mom." His blue eyes twinkled in the glow of the streetlamp. "I have to admit, I'm kind of shocked right now. Don't get me wrong, this is great news. I just never thought I'd see this day."

"That makes two of us. But God's all about giving us second chances. You got yours with Haven, and now your father and I are getting ours. It's a small miracle, but a miracle indeed."

"I'm really happy for you, Mom. I know this is what you always wanted."

She gave Jeremiah's cheek a soft pat. Her son was more aware of things than she'd realized. She used to think he and Jess were too young to understand the ramifications of a broken marriage, but now she knew better. "Thank you, dear. It really is."

"Hey, what did I miss?" Haven appeared at Jeremiah's side holding a full drink tray and a white paper bag. The scent of peppermint and chocolate wafted in the cold air between them. "Mom, you look great. I love your hat."

"Thank you, dear, I made it myself." Josephine had managed to crochet a simple red beanie this past week. "I was just telling Jeremiah that Jack has decided to move back to Freedom."

"Really? That's wonderful news!" Haven's cheeks turned a rosy pink as she bounced on the heels of her boots in excitement. "Miah's been praying for you and Dad every night, you know."

"I didn't know that." Josephine turned to Miah and pulled her in for another hug. "Thank you, sweetheart. God answered your prayers."

"I knew He would," she replied with a toothy smile. "He likes it when people love each other the way He loves us."

Josephine's heart warmed to witness Miah's pure faith. "You are absolutely right, Miah. How'd you get so wise?"

She shrugged and simply answered, "I was born wise."

The adults grinned and nodded in agreement.

Adam and Asher started jumping up and down as music came over the outdoor loudspeakers. "The tree!" they shouted. "We wanna see the tree! Let's go, Daddy!"

Jeremiah and Haven took the kids over to get a closer view of the ceremony as Josephine made her way over to Jan and Pete. Once she arrived at the bench, she took a seat beside Jan, eager to dig into the goodies her friend offered her.

"You've got to try this peppermint bark," Jan exclaimed. "It's delicious."

Josephine bit into a piece, savoring its rich, minty flavor. "It's so good. I love the heart shape. That's so creative."

"Isn't it? You should get some to share with Jack. You know, let him know how much you missed him while he was away."

Josephine grinned at the playful way Jan waggled her brows. "When did you get so romantic, Jan? I'm guessing you're to blame for this, Pete?"

"Guilty as charged," the man sitting on the other side of Jan remarked. The corners of his dark gray eyes crinkled as he laughed. "But to be fair, we rub off on each other. Jan brings out the best in me, and hopefully I in her."

"That you do, dear," Jan agreed. "That you do."

Josephine found it impossible to not smile at the sight of her two old friends making lovey-dovey eyes at one another. She hoped they didn't mind her tagging along as the third wheel since Titus, who was supposed to be her date for the night, was sick at home with a cold. Seeing Pete and Jan's affection for each other did make her long for Jack's return all the more. Jan was right, she did miss him an awful lot. It had only been a week since he'd left Freedom. Thankfully, he wouldn't be gone much longer.

"Now, inquiring minds want to know," Jan turned around to talk to Josephine, "have the two of you decided when the big day will be?"

"The big day as in the wedding day?" She rolled her eyes in amusement. "I think you're more eager than I am."

"In case you hadn't noticed, Jo, none of us are getting any younger."

"Believe me, I've noticed," Josephine remarked drolly as she pointed to her walker. "Jack said we'd talk about the future when he gets back. I'm sure he has marriage in mind. Whether or not there will be an actual wedding is yet to be determined. I don't think we need anything formal at our age, especially with this being our second rodeo. We could just as easily get married at City Hall."

"And deprive us all of a good celebration?" Jan balked. "Certainly not! How often do two people who fell out of love fall back in love? This calls for a party at least."

Josephine smiled. "You're wrong about that, Jan. I don't think either one of us ever fell out of love. We didn't like each other for a long while, that much is true, but we never stopped loving each other. You don't stop caring about your best friend just because they do something you don't agree with. You pray for God to work in both of your hearts and do your best to love him. And you stop yourself from saying anything in the heat of the moment that you'll regret." Her voice trailed off as she remembered all the things she'd ever done or said to hurt Jack. "If I could tell my younger self anything, it would be to keep my mouth shut and to listen more, really listen. Then I wouldn't have been so angry at Jack. I would've understood his intentions better."

Jan gave her arm a squeeze. "The important thing is that we're never too old to learn from our mistakes."

"So true." Josephine quirked a brow and joked, "Wait, are you calling me old?"

"You *are* four months older than me. That makes you wiser, too," she added with a wink.

"Only because I've had more time to make mistakes."

"Touché." Jan elbowed her playfully as they both burst out laughing.

Mayor Starling's jolly voice boomed over the speakers, announcing the countdown to the ceremony. Josephine, along with the rest of the crowd, watched in anticipation as the bright Christmas tree lights lit up the sky. In the distance, she spotted her grandkids lining up for their turn to hang an ornament on the tree. Her heart was truly full. It was a wonderful evening, other than the fact that Jack wasn't here to enjoy it with her.

"We're going to get some cocoa," Pete interrupted her thoughts as he stood up. "Would you like one, Josephine?"

"Sure, thanks."

She watched as Pete and Jan walked off hand in hand. Left alone on the bench, she resorted to watching the families around her. There were a couple of familiar faces and many new ones, but this town still gave her the same feeling of belonging. No wonder it was common for people who had left Freedom to eventually return. This had been true for her kids and now it was true for her and Jack. They had all come home.

Now if only Jack would be home in time for Christmas.

Josephine felt her phone vibrate in her pocket with an incoming call. She pulled it out, excitement filling her as soon as she spotted Jack's name on the screen. "Jack, I was just thinking about you!"

His chuckle sounded over the line. "Were you now? I was

thinking about you, too, Joey. How are you? Where are you at? It sounds busy over there."

"I'm at the tree lighting ceremony with Pete and Jan. Jeremiah and Haven are here with the kids. Titus couldn't make it though; he has the sniffles. No fever thankfully, but Jess wanted to keep him home."

"I see. I'm glad you're out with friends. Say hi to everyone for me, will you?"

"Of course. How are you, Jack?"

"I'm good, just tired from a busy week."

"Any word on when you'll be coming back?"

"That's actually the reason why I called." He cleared his throat. "I had a talk earlier with my boss over at headquarters. He really likes what I've done here this week. So much that he's made me an offer, a really amazing one."

Josephine's body tensed. She hadn't heard the details yet, but she already wondered if this offer could delay Jack's return. "What is it?"

"One of their medics is taking an extended leave. He asked if I could stay on longer and help fill that void for them."

She wrapped her arm around her middle, suddenly feeling cold, despite the thick winter coat she wore. "How long would that be for?"

"Three months, maybe up to six. But the best part is that I'll get a raise *and* a bonus if I stay. Isn't that amazing? They don't make this kind of offer to just anyone, Joey."

"That is amazing." Her words sounded strangled to her ears, but Jack didn't seem to notice. He was already going on about how Texas was only a two-hour flight away and he could come home every other weekend. It sounded like he was seriously considering this offer.

"What do you think, Joey? I wanted to discuss this with you first before giving him an answer."

"I-I don't know. This is a bit sudden. I thought you'd be coming home for Christmas." Saying this last line made her eyes well up, just like every other time she'd said it throughout her life. First to her parents, then to Jack. Each instance felt like a stab to her heart, but this one hurt her the most. She'd thought those days were behind her now. Apparently, she'd been wrong.

"I can be back for New Year's, well, the day after New Year's Day. I know it's not what we were planning, but think about it. We could use this extra money for our retirement. It's always good to have more in the bank."

She couldn't believe her ears. Why was it always about money? "But we have enough, Jack. I have more than enough saved up."

"I know you do, but I want to do my part. I want to support you, too. I don't want to have to rely on your inheritance."

"What do you mean? Now that we're back together, it's our money to use together. It's not just mine."

He grew quiet for a moment. "That money was always meant for you, Joey, and you alone. Your folks never wanted me to have a penny of it. I don't feel right using it."

Her throat constricted. She understood now what was going on. The disregard her parents had had for Jack still affected him to this day. That young teenage boy who hadn't felt good enough to date the Waltons' daughter still existed somewhere inside of him. And no matter how much she argued—she'd tried plenty of times in the past—she wouldn't be able to change his mind.

What do I do, God? How do I tell Jack it's never been about the money with him? What do I say that will convince him?

"I am the bread of life. Whoever comes to me will never go hungry, and whoever believes in me will never be thirsty." (John 6:35, NIV)

Josephine stilled. This verse came to mind, its words infusing a great deal of comfort into her heart. *Please help us understand this truth better, Lord,* she prayed. *And help me once again to be the friend and partner that Jack needs.*

With a peace that surpassed her understanding, she spoke what was in her heart. "Jack, if you feel the need to work longer, I won't stop you. But I want you to know that what's mine is yours. When you asked me to marry you when we were twenty and I said yes, I said yes to sharing everything with you—my life and my heart and everything in between. I still say yes to you now, and I'll keep saying yes for as long as the good Lord allows me to. I love you. You are more than enough for me. And I'll be waiting as long as I need to for you to come home."

She ended the call with tears streaming down her face. Was what she said enough? How long would she have to wait to see Jack again?

Part of her wanted to stew in her emotions and dwell on what had gone wrong, but she needed to have faith. Closing her eyes, she took a deep breath and chose to hold onto God's promises.

The moment she lifted her lashes, she saw Jeremiah running over with his phone in one hand.

"Mom! Jess is in labor. We gotta go!"

*J*ack sat in silence for a good five minutes, replaying Josephine's words in his mind.

I love you. You are more than enough for me. And I want you to know that I'll be waiting as long as I need to for you to come home.

It was almost like God was speaking to him through her. These sentiments were the spiritual truths that Jack needed once again to be reassured of.

He was loved.

He had enough.

And he needed to go home.

I hear You, Lord, he prayed. *I receive Your love and grace for me.*

Hot tears fell from his eyes as he allowed himself to finally lay down the burdens he'd been carrying around for most of his life. It was time to hand them over to the only One who could fulfill his soul's hunger and thirst. Instead of chasing momentary things that gave him a false and fleeting sense of security, Jack was ready to chase after what mattered the most—his relationship with God. Understanding his identity in the Lord—as a sinner saved by grace —would give him the confidence he needed, not to trust in what he could provide but in what God had already provided for him.

A great sense of peace washed over Jack as he wiped his face. He had an answer to give to Mason now and he was more than ready to return to Freedom. It was time to make some calls.

After packing up his belongings, he officially gave his notice to work. He also managed to find a last-minute airplane ticket and grab a lift off the rig with some crew members going ashore for the weekend. Within two hours, he was back at the airport ready to board his flight.

He placed a call to Josephine. Disappointment settled in his gut when her voicemail picked up. He tried to reach her again when he got on the plane, but there was no answer. Could she have already turned in for the night? Or was she so upset that she was avoiding his calls? Or had she gotten into trouble of some kind and couldn't come to the phone? His heart pounded as he considered all the possibilities.

He then remembered that she had gone to the tree lighting ceremony with Jan and Pete. He dialed his old friend's number.

"Jack?" Pete's gruff voice answered, sounding sleepy. "I didn't expect to hear from you."

"Hey Pete, sorry to call you so late."

"No worries. Jan and I were just about to turn in. We had a lot of sweets tonight downtown, and the sugar crash is about to take over. What's going on with you?"

"I'm trying to reach Josephine, but she's not answering my calls. Did you guys drop her off at home after the tree lighting?"

"No, she went with Jeremiah. She left us a message saying

Jess had gone into labor and she was going over to stay with Titus. That's the last we heard from her."

Jack's brows shot up. "Thanks, Pete. I gotta run, my plane's taking off now."

"You're coming back?"

"Yes, I'm on my way home. For good."

"It's about time! We'll see you back in Freedom."

Before he could call Josephine again, a young, dark-haired flight attendant motioned for him to put his phone away. "We're about to take off, sir. Thank you for your cooperation."

Jack switched his phone to airplane mode, then settled back in his seat. Excitement filled him to know that he was about to welcome another grandchild soon. Jess wasn't due for another couple of weeks though. He felt an urgency to pray for his daughter. Then he prayed for the rest of his family and for his friends and old colleagues, too. Each and every person he lifted up to the Lord held a special place in his heart, especially those in his hometown. After so many years of wandering, he was finally going home to where he belonged.

Nearly two hours later, his prayers came to an end when the pilot announced they were getting ready to descend into Denver. Jack opened his eyes to a dimly lit cabin and saw the same flight attendant from earlier walking around collecting trash. The scene was calm and quiet as passengers stared outside the windows at the skyline below. Jack exchanged a smile with the young mother and child sitting to his left and made some small talk, until a loud *thud* caught his attention. He glanced up to see that the white-haired man who had been sitting two rows in front of him had keeled over onto the floor.

The flight attendant rushed over and dropped to her

knees. "Sir! Sir, can you hear me? We need a doctor! Is there a doctor on board?! Someone get a doctor! Hurry!"

Jack sprang to his feet, quickly moving down the aisle to reach the man. "I'm a medic!" he announced as his instincts kicked in. "Let's clear the area and get him on his back."

As soon as Jack saw the man's ashen face and labored breathing, he knew they were dealing with a cardiac arrest. He immediately started CPR. Moments later a young man who identified himself as a first-year medical student jumped into alternate chest compressions with Jack.

Jack took the opportunity to speak with the flight attendant. "How long till we land?"

"About twenty minutes. Is he going to be okay?"

"I hope so. Let the pilot know we'll need emergency services to meet us on the ground. And please get me the AED."

The flight attendant brought him the bright yellow defibrillator device, which he attached to the man's chest. He quickly delivered the first shock. When no return of a pulse was detected, Jack and the med student continued CPR and used the AED again. He lost count of the number of times they went back and forth like this, but the one thing he continued doing all the while was pray for a miracle. This man and everyone witnessing this terrible event needed a miracle.

After what felt like an eternity, Jack finally saw the man's eyelids flutter. It was the sign of life he'd been waiting for! *Thank You, Lord!*

Color returned to the man's complexion, and he opened his eyes, looking bewildered.

"Can you tell me your name, sir?" Jack asked him.

"It's Bill. What happened?"

"You had a heart attack, but you're okay now. Try to lay

still. I'll stay with you until we land. Do you have someone we can call for you?"

The man was soon coherent enough to give him the name of his daughter who was picking him up at the airport. He also informed Jack of his medical history and the medications he was currently on. Jack took mental notes of all the information so he could relay it to the airport medics later.

By this time, the cabin pressure shifted as the plane's altitude continued to decrease. The mechanical sounds coming from underneath the floor signaled the activation of the landing gear. Jack held onto the man's shoulder and legs, securing him in place, as the plane made contact with the runway. A couple of bumps later, they came to a halt and began taxiing to the gate. Within minutes, an EMS crew was on board with a stretcher.

Before he was taken away, Bill grabbed ahold of Jack's hand and gave it a heartfelt squeeze. "I know God put you on this plane for a reason. Thank you for saving my life."

Jack returned his smile in wholehearted agreement. "It was my pleasure, Bill, but the real thanks go to God. Like you said, He had a purpose for me to be here. I almost didn't take this flight, but He convinced me to come home."

"I'm glad you listened to Him then."

"I am, too. You take care now," he added with one last wave at Bill.

Now that the worst was over, Jack wiped away the sweat along his temple and released a weary breath. His heart rate returned to normal as his adrenaline began to subside. He thanked the med student and flight attendant for their help. Several passengers clapped him on the back as he walked off the plane. The crew members, as well as the captain, spoke words of appreciation. News about the incident must have spread because once he stepped into the terminal, the people there met him with applause.

"What happened on the plane?"

"Are you the guy who saved the man's life?"

"You're a hero!"

"I just did what I knew how to do," Jack answered the passersby. "It was all God. He put me in the right place at the right time."

He shook his head. Wasn't that the absolute truth? The situation couldn't have worked out better. Jack was truly grateful that the Lord had used the step of faith he'd taken and turned it into a blessing for someone else.

He walked toward the exit with a renewed sense of purpose and security. Whatever the future held, he knew it was in God's hands. He just needed to put his trust in Him and do his part.

As for the present, all he wanted now was to be with his loved ones and to make up for lost time. He pulled out his phone, ready to make some calls, when he heard someone shout his name.

"Jack!"

His breath caught in his throat to see Josephine with her walker, waving to him from the glass sliding doors. He ran over, his feet moving in time to the rapid pace of his heartbeat, and wrapped the woman he loved up in his arms. "Joey! What are you doing here?"

"Pete called and told me you were flying back. I asked Jeremiah to drive me here." She pulled back and cupped his face. Her brows furrowed with concern. "I didn't expect you to come back so soon. Is everything okay? You look exhausted."

"I'm good. A lot happened on the plane, but I'll fill you in on that later. How's Jess? Did she have the baby yet?"

"She did! A little girl. Six pounds, fifteen ounces, and

nineteen and a half inches long. We can visit them in the morning."

"I'd like that. I'm ready to start my retirement and to spend it with you and our amazing family." He placed a kiss on the top of her head. "I've finally found the place where I belong, Joey. I'm back for good this time."

"You don't know how happy I am to hear that." Leaning in close, she nuzzled the tip of his nose with hers. Then she placed a tender, lingering kiss on his lips that warmed him to the core. "Welcome home, Jack, welcome home."

EPILOGUE

This Christmas really was turning out to be the best one of her life.

Josephine couldn't stop beaming as she looked about the large conference room at Freedom Ridge Lodge. Haven and her staff had done an outstanding job of decorating the place for her and Jack's "coming-back party." That's what Miah called this celebration of theirs, which Josephine agreed was the perfect term to use. She and Jack had not only come back to their hometown but also to one another. By the grace of God, they were once again Mr. and Mrs. Gilbert. They had gone down to City Hall a few days ago and made it official.

Being remarried to her first and only love had once seemed like an impossible dream, but here they were holding hands under the white linen tablecloth at their table for two. Ever since Jack returned from Texas, they'd been learning how to reintegrate their lives with each other's, starting with their living arrangements. His clothes now took up half of her closet since he moved into her apartment, but she didn't mind at all. After being on her own for so long, she loved the idea of sharing her space. She appreciated Jack's presence and company even more.

"You look like you're enjoying yourself," Jack murmured as he brought her hand to his lips for a kiss. He looked so handsome in a navy suit that matched the sequined dress she wore. "Have I told you how beautiful you look today?"

"Only a dozen times." Josephine's cheeks warmed. "You look pretty good yourself, hometown hero."

"Don't you start with that, too." He chuckled. "I still can't believe I made the front page of the Gazette this week. It must've been a slow news day."

"What you did was very newsworthy, Jack." When Jack had told her what had happened on the plane ride from Dallas, she had been moved to tears at how God had worked everything together for good. "I'm so proud of you, not only because you saved a man's life. I'm proud of the man you've become. I'm so thankful I get to be by your side again after all these years."

"Me, too. It's been a wild ride, hasn't it?" He glanced around the room at the other tables where their family and friends sat. Jan and Pete were among the attendees as were some new friends from the hospital. "Who would've thought we'd be sitting here together today?"

"God knew," she answered with a grin. "And apparently Miah did, too."

She looked over at the adjacent table where their granddaughter sat in between her brothers. Josephine couldn't believe their children were now grown with children of their own. God had blessed them so much. It was such a meaningful moment to have them all in one room, including little Tabitha who was now a week old. Seeing the grandchildren dressed up in their Sunday best with their little hands holding the gold flatware was such a treat.

"That reminds me," Jack spoke up as he turned toward

Miah. "I haven't forgotten about our sledding date, Miah. We'll pick a day this week, okay?"

"Okay!" The toothy grin she flashed at them lit up her whole face. "We can pull Granny together!"

"That's a great idea. Did you hear that, boys?" Jack asked their grandsons. "Make sure you eat all your veggies, so you'll have plenty of strong muscles for sledding."

Adam raised his arms and shouted, "Yay, sledding!"

Asher chimed in with a loud, "Sledding!"

Titus nodded readily, his full cheeks resembling a hamster's.

The rest of the family sitting at the table laughed.

"Haven, you outdid yourself," Josephine remarked to her daughter-in-law. "Thank you for pulling this together at the last minute."

"I'm so glad you like it, Mom. This was definitely my favorite event to plan, aside from Jeremiah's and my wedding, of course," she added with a smile aimed at her husband.

"Haven had so much fun planning this party, she's already talking about doing it again next Christmas." Jeremiah grinned. "I think you guys may have started a new family tradition."

"That's not a bad idea," Josephine said thoughtfully. "What do you think, Jack? Should we do this every year?"

"For sure. I'd never turn down the chance of getting together with our friends and family."

"Yes!" Haven exclaimed. "With this much advance notice, I can reserve the ballroom for next year."

Josephine frowned. "Won't that be a bit much? I don't think we'll have enough people to fill such a big space."

"What about all the folks we'll meet playing Bingo this year?" Jack's eyes lit up with humor. "Not to mention all the people at church who will be giving us an earful when they find out we didn't invite them today."

"Good point, Jack. All right. As long as people show up, we'll be happy to host them."

"That's the spirit, Mom!" Jess, who was sitting between Jeremiah and Duncan, piped up. "Speaking of hosting, who wants to hear some words from our hosts? Come on, Mom and Dad! It's time for a speech!"

The room resounded with shouts of *Speech, speech, speech,* as the guests echoed Jess's request.

Jack turned to Josephine with an outstretched hand. "Shall we?"

She followed his lead up to the front of the room where a small podium stood. As Josephine looked out at all the familiar, smiling faces, her heart warmed at their show of support. She could hardly contain the feeling of awe and wonder that filled her. "Mind if I go first?" she asked Jack.

"By all means." He leaned the mic toward her.

"Thank you all so much for coming today," Josephine began. "Let me begin by saying that God is a God of miracles. Just the fact that Jack and I are here together is proof of that because you all know how stubborn I can be. It's even more true the older I get," she quipped to the sound of everyone's laughter. "But I've come to see that the Lord is so much more persistent than I am. His timing is perfect, too. He brought us back together after we'd both done some much-needed changing and growing."

"In more ways than one as you can see," Jack added, pointing to the gray in his hair.

"That's for sure," she replied with an easy chuckle. "But there are many things that haven't changed. Jack is still the same boy I fell in love with. His heart for people and for the Lord is still the same. He still makes me laugh like no one else can. And he knows me and accepts me despite all my imperfections. We may not have had a public ceremony this time around, but I want to declare to everyone here that I will love and cherish Jack Gilbert for the rest of my days." She turned to Jack and restated her vows, "I do again."

Without missing a beat, he wrapped an arm around her waist and pulled her close. His amber eyes darkened with intensity as he declared, "I vow to love and cherish you, Josephine Gilbert, for the rest of my days. You are the only woman for me, always have been and always will be. I do again, too."

The room hushed as the two of them got caught up in the moment, acting more like young newlyweds than seniors. They only broke off their stare when a young voice exclaimed, "Come on, Grandad, what are you waiting for? Give Granny a kiss!"

Jack glanced over at Miah and winked. "With pleasure!"

Then with a swift move, Jack dipped Josephine back, cradling her in his strong arms. A soft gasp of surprise escaped her lips, only to be replaced by a murmur of delight when Jack placed his mouth on hers. She rested in his embrace, soaking in every taste of his love for her.

That's when she knew. She'd been alone without her friends and family for far too long. But just like Jack, she had found her way home, back to where she belonged. What a sweet homecoming this was. One full of love, hope, and grace and the most wonderful gift of all, a second chance with her hero.

* * *

READY FOR MORE? Return to Freedom Ridge in *Inspired by the Hero*, the next book in the Heroes of Freedom Ridge series.

· · ·

Can a Blizzard be a Blessing?

CASEY CRAWFORD KNOWS how the town of Freedom, Colorado feels about her and her family. She's heard the whispers and knows they have no more use for her than they have for AC in December.

So, when she gets trapped in a chalet in the woods with the object of her secret crush and he shows interest in her, she knows it can't lead to happily-ever-after. He'll eventually see that the Crawfords are nothing but trouble, and if she doesn't get him killed first, she'll ruin his reputation.

GAGE BUCHANAN HAS HAD his share of trouble, and isn't looking for more, but when he offers Casey a ride home from work, someone starts shooting at them. He can't leave a damsel in distress to her own devices, and the more time they spend together the more she finds her way into the cracks in the wall he's built up around his heart.

HE KNOWS she deserves better than him, but if she keeps turning those trusting blue eyes his way, he won't be able to keep himself from wishing they could be more than friends. In order for that to happen, he has to keep her alive and figure out why someone wants her dead. He plans to do just that, but there are forces at work he can't control, but God can, if he'll turn to Him.

.   .   .

DON'T MISS out on any of the books in this beloved series! Check them all out on our Heroes of Freedom Ridge series page.

* * *

Join in all the fun at our Facebook Reader Group
www.facebook.com/groups/freedomridgereaders
For sneak peeks, giveaways, and tons of Christmas romance fun!

ABOUT THE AUTHOR

Liwen Y. Ho works as a chauffeur and referee by day (AKA being a stay at home mom) and an author by night. She writes sweet and inspirational contemporary romance infused with heart, humor, and a taste of home (her Asian roots).

In her pre-author life, she received a Master's degree in Marriage and Family Therapy from Western Seminary, and she loves makeovers of all kinds, especially those of the heart and mind. She lives in the San Francisco Bay Area with her techie husband and their two children.

Sign up for Liwen's newsletter to receive an exclusive free book, news about her upcoming releases, giveaways, sneak peeks, and more at: http://liwenho.com/free-book.

ACKNOWLEDGMENTS

I'd like to thank the following people who blessed me in the writing of this book:

My lovely ARC readers—I am truly grateful you took time out of your busy lives to read and review this book!

My critique partners, Kristen Iten and Jocelyn Fitch, who are the most invaluable work buddies an author could have!

My awesome proofreader Regina Dowling—I so enjoy working with you!

My wonderful hubby and munchkins—thank you for your behind-the-scenes support.

My Lord and Savior who gave me the words, as well as the life lessons I needed, to write this story.

And you, my dear reader, for taking a visit to our beloved little town of Freedom. I hope you enjoyed your time there!

The Spark Brothers: A Christian Contemporary Romance Collection

A tight-knit family of five amazing brothers and the women who challenge and delight them. Five full-length novels in one wonderful collection.

Why reviewers love the Spark brothers:
"These Spark brothers sure do set a girl's heart on fire."

"I absolutely LOVE this series. This is an awesome family of five brothers all who have a strong faith."

"I know I enjoy books when they feel real and after this series, I wish the Spark brothers were real. Thank you, Liwen Y. Ho, for writing stories to remind me that God wastes nothing and is always at work. Now please excuse me while I go reread the series."

A Single Spark (Book One): A pop singer running from his past. A deejay who's given up on men. Will the sparks igniting between them end up in flames or romance?

A Sudden Spark (Book Two): A writer too shy to speak to women. A single mom who's sworn off men. Will a marriage of convenience end their friendship or spark a lasting romance?

The Sweetest Spark (Book Three): A fun-loving ice cream shop owner looking for more than a fling. A straight-laced food critic too scared for love. Will an accident be the spark that drives them apart for good or gives them their sweetest taste of romance yet?

At First Spark (Book Four): A tender-hearted firefighter who's been burned by love. An optimistic bookstore owner determined to heal his heart. Will the spark that drew them to each other be enough to keep their love burning or will their short-lived romance go down in flames?

An Extra Spark (Book Five): An actor pressured to risk everything for his job. An actress struggling to fit into the Hollywood scene. Will the hazards of show business spark new insecurities or strengthen their bond of trust?

Grab your copy on Amazon and fall in love with the Spark brothers today!